Chaos Ending

Gwydion Royce

ORACLE OF LOST PATHS BOOKS

CHAPTER ONE

Meg

"What is this?" I demanded. "Where are we?"

Maat stood there so casually, arms crossed over her chest with a hip cocked to the side. She said nothing.

I moved closer to the ghoulish scene, peering through the shadows of the cloaks and hoods of the three figures. This had to be a trick. Another one. There's no way...

The three desiccated eyes stuck to the spindle seemed to glare at me accusingly. The figure seated at the wheel still had a thread stuck between shriveled, mummified fingers, gone a dark gray-purple. I moved aside the heavy woolen cloth of the hood, easing it down around the figure's shoulders. Wispy white hair was still attached to the skull in a few places, but most of it came away with the hood, revealing leathery skin covered with wobbly black lines that might've been tattoos a long time ago.

The face looked like you would expect, except for the deep sunken ridge where the missing eyes would've been. Her mouth was opened in surprise, like she'd only been given a second to realize a trusted friend was there to murder her.

The other two mummies were the same, one holding shears and the other, an unused spindle. Only Atropos, the Fate that cut the cord of life, had recognized what was coming. Her face twisted with eternal fury, the shears held like a weapon in front of her, with a dry, reddish smear staining the ends. At least she'd gotten a piece of their attacker.

Maat was still watching me, but that smug satisfaction was fading. Her shoulders rose with tension, inching toward her ears as the arms crossing her chest became a self-soothing hug. Pain pulled at the corners of her eyes and Ammit moved closer, protective of his mistress.

"Please," I said. "Tell me something."

"It's seldom that I visit the seven hells," she said, quietly enough that I imagined it was more of a comment to herself than to me.

"What happened?" I had to move away from them, taking a few steps toward Maat. "How does nobody know about this?"

Even the Titans had been sure it was the Fates that were guiding us. Watching over my creation, ensuring that this journey continued. That it would be me and my mates standing at the gates of Tartarus when this was all over.

"We were on the same side, you know. All they had to do was adjust a few things. Tip the scales every now and again. We kept the balance, regardless." The bitterness coating her words made *my* face pucker. She moved close enough to the bodies to give them each a hard look. "I've never seen them up close. I'd only heard—"

A breeze blew through the cavern and rattled the wheel, making the Fates' cloaks move with sudden life. Maat jumped back and cursed herself for getting spooked. She spun back to me and snapped her fingers, bringing us back to the giant scales and my mates, still frozen in place.

A sharp rap of her hands had them all stumbling forward with grunts, gasps and a few choice words.

"Meg," said Andrus, hurrying over to me, followed quickly by the others, although Hadi lingered in the back and Gareth kept his distance, watching Maat closely.

"The Fates," I said, glancing back at Maat. "They're dead."

Shocked silence. "You saw them?" asked Felix.

I nodded, throat tight as I spoke. "Maat thought she'd set the record straight." They all turned toward the goddess, who still looked haunted by what she'd seen.

Hadi stepped forward, far more comfortable questioning an Ætherim from the pantheon he dealt with daily. "Lady, please explain. It's clearly weighing on you."

Maat's eyes lingered on Gareth, but all thoughts of wooing him had evaporated. She couldn't help taking one last jab at me, though. "The construct speaks the truth."

"How is that possible?" asked Hadi.

"It happened"—she sought around in her memory, but waved a hand in dismissal—"a long time ago. The Ætherim had begun to get pushback by monotheists. Our worshipers were dying or leaving the old ways behind. It did not affect our power any, but... the change in lifestyle was significant. Many of us had to settle for small cult worship, or give up altogether and let our temples fall entirely. For some, it wasn't an issue, but others weren't willing to accept that loss of control. To become classified as a *myth*. To walk on this earth as a powerful being but get no recognition for it."

She narrowed her eyes as she read the room. "You can save your judgment, I know what I sound like. But until you've been treated with godly status, you have no idea what it means to lose it."

"Where do the Fates fit into this?" Remi asked.

Maat turned the full weight of her scornful glare on him. "Patience, gargoyle." Remi's wings flicked at the ends in annoyance, the snapping sound sharp as it echoed around the room.

"When chaos came, it seemed like a splendid opportunity. It would give us a chance to regain our power."

I gasped, the pieces falling into place. "And when you say 'chaos,' you mean—"

She nodded. "The demons just appeared. No one realized they were still around, figuring they'd faded or become casualties of the Titan wars. They didn't want to choose a side any more than the Titans did."

"What could they have offered you that would've sounded appealing?" I asked, horrified.

She sneered. "Humans are feeble things. That they had more control over the world than we did, that they could affect *our* lives as much as they had, was an insult most of us couldn't contend with. Adding some chaos to the situation would bring them to their knees, crawling back to our worship. Begging us to save them."

I huffed a laugh. "How'd that work out for you? You probably made them more zealous."

She shot me a withering glare. "Hindsight. We didn't think what the chaos demons would get out of the deal. They got their upheaval, and by the time any of us wanted to step in to stop it, it was far too late. The damage was done. When they relinquished their hold, we swept it away. Another dirty little secret."

"But they didn't let go, did they?" Felix asked.

Maat shook her head. "No. But that isn't widely known, even among the Ætherim. There were a few of us, mostly those that twisted fates, kept balances, meted out justice. We knew. The demons came to us in secret with a plan to keep their good deal going without anyone else being the wiser." She sighed. "All we had to do was tip things in their favor, not even that often. Where we would seek order, sometimes things became a little disorderly. Rarely was it outrageous."

"They wouldn't need anything significant," said Hadi. "One little change can have catastrophic effects down the line." I could tell he was struggling to keep his temper in check. His own pantheon, that he'd sworn his life to, was guilty of this kind of treachery. "You of all people should know that."

Maat's eyes flashed with anger before she admitted the truth. Her posture deflated. "Yes. But it was easy."

"The Fates didn't want to cooperate," I said.

"No," she said, a small smile quirking her lips. "They refused. I wasn't there for the confrontation, but I heard about it."

The smile vanished. "Seeing it, however... I don't think I've ever felt more shame than I do right now." Her eyes flicked to me. "I thought it would be a good way to teach you a lesson. I guess that backfired, too."

"Are the chaos demons still in charge? Still twisting fate as they want it?" Felix asked.

"I haven't heard from them in a long while," she said, stroking Ammit's flank.

Gareth's face darkened. "It seems safe to assume we're all going to be hearing from them very soon."

Chapter Two

Meg

The rest of the night passed in a blur. Even as the festivities of the Feast of Opet continued, the allure was no longer there. I was in a daze. While Hadi took a little more time to come to terms with his leaving, I sat in the inner temple at Karnak with the others, staring into a crackling fire and ignoring the surrounding conversations.

Every blow dealt to us before now seemed insignificant. This changed everything. The Titans hadn't even known. My very existence was in question. If the Fates were dead, there could be no doubt who was ultimately responsible for my being here.

Chaos—the god—was, in essence, my grandfather. But the chaos demons were something else. There was nothing cosmic or primordial about them, nothing serene or ethereal. They were abominations of leftover energy that coalesced into creatures one day and wreaked havoc everywhere they set foot.

When Hadi rejoined us from saying his goodbyes, I drew time around us and off we went to Death's house. The minute we reappeared, I walked away. I couldn't stomach any of this right now.

"Meg," Andrus said, following me.

I held up my hand. "I'll be alright, I just need some time."

He took another step toward me. "Alone," I snapped, hating myself for the look of hurt on his face. "I'm sorry," I muttered, hurrying away.

"No," said Hadi.

Power laced through the words, but it wasn't a command. He was imploring me to stay.

I stopped, dumbfounded, and turned back to him, locking eyes with Hadi as he crossed the distance and stopped in front of me. His eyes were as tremulous as I felt, and a tongue of flame sizzled around his body before twisting around me.

Mine, it said with velvet-tongued warmth. *Stay.*

"You shouldn't be alone," he said.

"I—"

He lifted his hand and grazed my chin with his thumb. "Please. Let us help you."

My breath shuddered as I fought with the rising anxiety. Hadi held out his hand, and I took it. As he led me over to the others, Death came into the room, followed by Arthur.

Arthur and Hadi shared a brief smile and clasped hands, but Arthur looked sad for his own reasons.

"Welcome back," said Death, but he paused when he noticed the somber tone in the room. "What's happened?"

This was supposed to be the pivotal moment. All members of the Six were reunited. We could set out and complete the mission with which we'd been charged. Off we'd go to save the day.

My mates looked at me to deliver the news. "The Fates are dead. Have been for a long time."

Death blinked. "What?"

Gareth told the story until it got to the part where Maat transported me to the cave. Hadi was standing by my side, arm around my shoulder, and the amount of body heat he gave off was immense. It was like standing next to a furnace, but I wasn't complaining. Recounting the story chilled my blood, and he took the edge off it.

"That is—" Death swiped a hand through his hair before sitting heavily on the couch he conjured out of thin air underneath him. "Damn."

"You all realize what this means, right?" I asked.

Seven pairs of eyes looked back at me, but nobody had an answer. "Chaos demons are the epitome of trouble. The foundation of everything bad that happens in the world." My hands trembled. "And now I find out that they were the ones that guided *my* creation?"

A shock of alarm went through the bond. I snorted softly. "Didn't think about that one, did you?"

Hadi grabbed my hands and squeezed them tight to stop them shaking. His warmth spread though me, and I breathed. "They took the Titans' essences—the best parts of themselves that they sacrificed and offered up to be made into the key to their escape—and the demons twisted them into something of their own design. Can I even trust myself?"

I felt like a bomb waiting to go off. Was there some kind of trigger word that would suddenly unleash the apocalypse through me? Would I turn on my mates? Were the Titans fooling us all and would releasing them be the ultimate coup for chaos?

"While the involvement of chaos demons makes a lot of sense in the grander scheme of the world," said Death, "I have to say that that is, without a doubt, the dumbest thing I've ever heard you say."

I blinked as I processed what he'd said. Gareth and Andrus grunted with agreement and when I shot them a glare, Andrus shrugged, a grin tugging at his stoic face. "I love you, but he's got a point. You're letting those punk demons get in your head."

"Weren't you just going on about how, even if the Titans and the Fates intended a certain outcome, how you get there is up to you?" asked Felix.

"Yeah, but—"

"And when we discussed what happened to my family, and I was bound and determined to walk away from all of you because I deemed myself unworthy, you were the one who convinced me I shouldn't define myself by my past. Especially when certain things were out of my control," said Remi.

"Well, yeah, but—" I tried again.

Gareth chuckled. "I'm not sure if you've noticed, but things have been hectic and generally fucked since we started on this journey. Nothing has gone right, but we still pull it together. You thrive under pressure."

He held up a hand to stave off my protest. "It's not enjoyable by any stretch of the imagination, but you still rise above it, every time. I'm kind of tempted to think that being guided by chaos was actually a boon for you. For all of us."

"Some boon," I murmured.

Hadi was staring at me, all but expressionless and yet still eliciting some reaction deep within me, like he was calling to me.

"You are very intense," I said.

He blinked, the corners of his eyes crinkling with a soft smile. "I'm sorry. I was simply trying to figure out how a woman that brought me to my knees is now so hesitant, even fearful of herself."

My cheeks flamed. "Well... I..." But I had nothing. He was right. They all were. It didn't matter what forces or circumstances made me. For the longest time, I thought it was pure dumb luck that I developed a mind of my own. I held onto the beliefs that I was nothing but a construct and the only way I would ever get my independence is if I helped Bel destroy the Titans. But I was wrong.

Once I stopped holding on so tight to the negative thoughts and doubt—mostly because things were moving so fast that I didn't even have time to think about them—I began to truly come into my power. Into myself. Even the last bits of hesitation with my mates and the worries that plagued me about how real our love was were completely unfounded.

I steadied myself. What's done was done. Nothing mattered but putting one foot in front of the other. Everything else was just noise. And self-doubt. And anxiety...

But one look around at my mates and that all faded away. Six amazing men were watching me with the compassion and love (mostly) I never could've dreamed of finding. Yes, we fell hard and fast, but that didn't make it any less genuine, not after everything we'd been through.

And even though things had gone off the rails substantially and they'd suffered with me through the majority, Gareth and

Andrus were still standing by me, steadfast as ever. My relationships were deepening with the others with every passing day. We were making this work.

Then I realized who I'd overlooked in my overwhelm.

"Where's Sasha?" I asked, glancing at Death. He wouldn't have actually *removed her* from the picture, right? The look of annoyance Death shot back was answer enough.

Arthur's face fell. "She left. Sasha decided she didn't want to risk getting in the way, especially if the chaos demon is planning on using her as a weapon. She wants to explore what the world has to offer."

A world without him. "I'm sorry," I said, and meant it. It was difficult to see him in pain, even though I was grateful Sasha had bowed out. Knowing what I do now... I was convinced she was being used as a pawn, or worse.

He nodded his head, the scruff on his face and the weariness in his eyes aging him about twenty years.

"There are many things we need to discuss, it seems," said Hadi, watching the interaction with confusion.

"Why don't you all get some rest, and we'll discuss next steps in the morning?" asked Death, rising to his feet. The sofa disappeared. "The sooner I can get my house back, the better."

"You don't like having seven impromptu guests filling the place with drama?" I asked.

He cast me a baleful look, and I chuckled.

After a vain attempt at settling in for the night, the thought of spending it alone was too much. I wandered through the halls, hoping to find a distraction or the kitchens, but the light was still on in one of the rooms and I felt Andrus's signature in there. I knocked lightly on his door.

You never need to knock, love.

I smiled and went in. "Hearing you in my head is becoming less and less shocking. I kind of like the mind-meld now."

He held out his arm and I snuggled up next to him, resting against his chest as he read a book about military campaigns.

"Does your brain ever turn off?" I teased.

"Never," he said, kissing the top of my head before turning a page. I was just dozing off when another knock sounded at the door.

"Gareth," Andrus said, snorting, sensing his signature the same way I had his. "Come in," he called.

The door cracked open and Gareth popped in, eyes closed. "Everybody decent? I can come back later."

"All clear," I said, yawning and rubbing my eyes.

His eyes popped open and then widened in surprise. "Wow. Honeymoon's over already? You're just quietly reading when you have an entire bed to yourselves?"

"Too tired for anything else," I said, yawning again, even though with Gareth wearing only boxer-briefs, I was tempted to examine his tattoos further.

"I didn't get a chance to apologize earlier, for Maat," he said, taking a few steps into the room.

"That wasn't your fault," I said.

He shook his head. "Regardless, I couldn't let it go the night without talking to you about it." He grinned. "I looked for you in your room first, to be clear. There was no intent on busting into a private moment, I swear."

"Can you blame Maat?" I asked. "Nothing she said about you was wrong. And you would make a cute couple."

Gareth scratched the back of his head with an awkward smile and shrugged. "My charm strikes again. It's always getting me in trouble."

Andrus closed his book. "Yeah, the *charm* is what did it. Nothing to do with you walking in there with your Big Wolf energy."

Gareth took a minute to calculate what Andrus had said while I tried to hold back my laughter. I would never tire of hearing modern terms come out of the mouths of men that had been stuck in the distant past.

When he understood, he chuckled, the warm, rich sound unwinding more of my stress.

"Maybe that, too," Gareth conceded.

Andrus had noticed the additional drop in my anxiety, and he motioned for the wolf to close the door. "Why don't you join us?"

Gareth raised an eyebrow. "Are you sure? If you two want time alone—"

"It's fine with me," said Andrus, looking at me.

I smiled, grateful. "I'd like that."

Gareth climbed into bed on my other side and Andrus turned out the light. I fell asleep quickly, cocooned in their arms.

CHAPTER THREE

Hadi

"What do you mean, we can't just travel there? Meg already did it once," said Felix.

"That was under specific circumstances, and she didn't travel there bodily," said Death.

I watched the interaction with my usual detachment. It wasn't my place to speak yet. There were many things for me to learn, catch up on. Remi had filled me in on the lion's share of the happenings and gotten me caught up with most of it, but there were too many blanks for me to feel confident about contributing.

A dragon never wastes words.

Death seemed altogether put-out by Felix. I couldn't say for sure that the dark elf was being thickheaded on purpose, but it certainly wasn't below him. I wasn't sure how Death appeared to Felix, but to me, the egregore appeared with a long black beard and thick, braided hair with a severely pointed face and fire burning in his eyes. He was more a compilation of notable figures in my past rather than a reproduction of any one in particular, but I still wouldn't have wanted to see the look on his face directed at me.

"The only option is to make the journey through all seven realms of hell?" asked Remi, incredulous. "That can't be what the Titans planned."

"Why not?" asked Meg. "To them it would seem like a walk in the park. They have the kind of power that they could walk through every circle with no fear of what they'd come across. It wouldn't have crossed their minds, like so many other things never did."

Her voice was bitter, and it was justified. I owed my life to the Titans, and I was devoted to them wholly, but their shortsightedness in the small details was difficult to swallow.

They had always seemed like shining beacons of wisdom, the powerful creators that would fix the world's ills. But while they were wise, and great, and good, their power hampered their judgment. All their careful planning didn't stand for much when it came down to it.

Beings that powerful could *only* see the bigger picture. It was just the world they lived in.

Death shook his head, braid swaying across the backs of his shoulders. "You're not completely out of luck. I can get you all the way to the Drop, but that's only the fourth realm. You'll have to make it past the Watcher on your own."

I'd been watching Meg, studying her reactions, but at the mention of the Watcher, I tore my attentions away.

"The Watcher?" Gareth asked.

"The guardian with a thousand eyes," I said.

Everyone turned to me in surprise.

"You have experience with him?" Death asked, folding his long arms.

I nodded. "It was part of the initiation into my priestly order. It was only soul travel, not in our physical bodies, but we had to seek him out. He holds the keys to unlocking any secret or doorway, to attaining the knowledge of the universe or just knowing yourself. The only problem is getting that information from him. I had been tasked with finding Osiris."

"Osiris?" Meg asked.

I hummed. "He'd gone on a journey of his own, to recuperate. But when he didn't come back after a century, people began to worry."

"Did you find him?" she asked.

"Yes. But he wasn't ready to return." I left it at that and cocked my head to the side. "The Watcher is relatively benevolent, but I'm not sure if he has an allegiance. If he approves of our mission, he'll let us pass, but..."

"Are you implying we might have to fight a thousand-eyed beast?" Felix asked.

I shot him a glare. "If you call him a beast, you most certainly will."

Felix glared at me, but let the matter drop.

"So we only have to venture through three realms?" Meg asked.

"Four," said Death. "Tartarus is below the seventh realm."

"The Watcher's realm," said Remi, ticking them off on his fingers. "Shadow, Hekate's Gate and what else?"

"Shadow?" Meg looked around quizzically and shook her head. "Not to make anyone nervous that I don't know this already."

"Shadow is the realm of lost souls. They can't work off their karmic debts in Hell because their minds are shattered," explained Gareth.

"Sounds nice," said Meg, grimacing.

"Hekate's Gate is Lady Hekate's realm," Death said, a reverence in his voice.

"Isn't she a Titan?" Meg asked.

"Yes, but she was given special status by Zeus, as soon as he established his pantheon as one of the major powers among the Ætherim, and himself as one of the supreme rulers. He gave her a place of honor, and she was venerated among the gods. Even Belsioch didn't dare tangle with her," said Andrus.

"What did she do?" Meg asked.

"Dealt the definitive blow that ended the Ancients' reign," said Arthur. "She's one of the most powerful chthonic deities. She severed the Ancients' ties with the darkness of the underworld, which limited their power and allowed the gods to seal them away."

"And she's kept her distance from Kronos and the rest, even before all this went down. She didn't want anything to do with their wars," said Remi.

Meg lapsed into thoughtful silence.

"The realm of the Forsaken is the last," said Death. "Where the truly heinous souls that can't be redeemed go to wither." He visibly shuddered. "On the rare occasion that I have to deliver someone there, the experience lingers." He held up his hand after shooting Remi a dirty look. "And before you say it, yes, *I* can travel there, but the Watcher and Hekate know me and allow me to move freely between."

"Allow you?" Gareth asked, raising an eyebrow.

Death blew out a breath. "There are a few beings that exist that I have a healthy respect for, and I wouldn't deign to tread on their territory for anything. I will send you to the Watcher's realm and you're on your own from there."

"What can we do to prepare?" Meg asked. "I feel like we're still flying blind. And there's the small matter of figuring out how to undo the damage I did when I left my signature on the gates."

Andrus looked at Arthur. "Now that we have Arthur back, that should solve the situation, right? His lucky streak can break through anything."

Arthur looked uncomfortable. "It should."

"Why do I feel you're about to give us bad news?" said Gareth.

"I've been trying to access my power, but it won't come. I was hoping it was some side effect of coming back from the dead, but..." He looked at Death, who raised his hands in surrender.

"Don't look at me," he said. "You're back in your original body, there shouldn't be anything standing in the way of your gifts."

"Meg?" Arthur asked. She looked at him warily, like she was expecting him to lay blame on her, and I got irrationally angry at Arthur at the thought.

"Did anything go differently when you joined me back up with my memories?" he asked.

She shook her head, some stray strands of hair escaping from her braid. "No. It was the same as with Felix."

"Could it be your confidence is off?" Felix asked, voice muted.

Arthur blinked and looked at his closest companion. A hint of something—guilt, maybe—appeared in the tight set of his shoulders. "What do you mean?"

"Sasha threw you off, just admit it," said Felix. "She left you, and all that bullshit you were spewing about it being 'meant to be' that she was back was revealed for the lies you were telling yourself."

As the hostility in the room ratcheted up, I rolled my shoulders, determined not to get in the middle.

"I—" Arthur tried, but the words to defend himself wouldn't come.

"Again, stop and think," said Felix. "Maybe this is just what the demons wanted. Our ace in the hole to be so bound up in his self-doubt that his gift would become useless, and we'd all be shit out of luck."

"It's not a bad theory," Andrus agreed, Remi nodding along.

Arthur was straining to remain calm under the scrutiny, but he was starting to crack. "That might be the case, but I can't just turn it off. With more time—"

"We don't have more time!" snapped Felix. "You need to pull your head out of your ass! Your wife is dead and gone, and the thing that came back in her place is nothing but trouble. To sabotage us!"

"Felix," said Meg. It wasn't said in anger or reprimand, just a quiet intonation. Felix stopped. Meg reached out and grabbed his hand and I watched with sudden fascination as he calmed and sat on the arm of the couch beside her. He leaned into her touch and the look on his face said it all. He cared for her.

I never thought I'd see the day.

"Would this be a good time to bring up the small matter of bonding?" Death asked. "These trials will be taxing enough without *that* separation being a factor. You'll need to function as a single unit."

All eyes turned to Arthur once again.

"I don't know if I can," he said, helpless. He was being honest.

The others started in on him, but Meg silenced them. "Is there another way?"

"What do you mean?" asked Death. "A different way to bond with Arthur?"

Meg nodded. "As long as he wants it, that is."

Arthur sighed. "I do. I want the bond." His eyes fixed firmly on the floor. "But it still feels like a betrayal to Sasha if I go to bed with you."

I expected a further outburst, but the men deferred to their mate, and my fire roiled within me as I corrected myself. Soon, she would be my mate as well. Meg felt the intensity of my gaze and caught my eye briefly, blushed bright red, and looked away.

"Is there an alternative?" she asked again.

He considered. "Yes. It's not nearly as strong, and the added bonus of you gaining a new ability probably wouldn't happen, but you'd be able to communicate and share power through the link."

"Then we do that," said Meg, with no hesitation.

Death looked like he might argue the point, but changed his mind. "Very well," he sighed. "I'll see what I can put together."

Gareth shook his head and walked away before his temper got the best of him.

Chapter Four

Bel

I opened my eyes with a groan and was met with darkness. Not the kind of all-consuming darkness of a moonless night, but that dim shadow, like somebody had closed the blinds over the sun. The ground underneath me was cold and hard, with several rocks sticking into my back.

I sat up to get a better scope of my surroundings, and my head pounded so hard my vision blurred. Where was I? How had I gotten here?

The last thing I remembered was standing in Hades's house with Dendra, Meg's throat grasped in my hand as I worked out an escape plan. Now, I was naked and alone, in a strange place I didn't recognize.

When I stood, my headache became a splitting migraine, and my stomach lurched. My vision blacked out, and I woke again on the ground, a puddle of vomit by my head.

After taking several minutes to compose myself, I sat up much more slowly. Searching my memory was only turning up gaps. I grasped my chest as forgotten anguish echoed, but over what?

First things first. I closed my eyes and listened, first pushing past the pounding of my heartbeat, then the rushing of blood, until I could focus on my environment.

A gentle breeze blowing through dry leaves or grass. The creaking of dead branches, about ready to break. Perhaps water far in the distance, but it blended in so well with the wind it was hard to tell. I heard no birdsong, no scuffling of animals or larger beasts. My eyes snapped open as an echoing wail carried through the darkness, gone as abruptly as it started, sending fear racing up my spine. I'd never heard a sound like that before.

Forcing myself back into a state of calm—I'd be damned if I let fear get the better of me after all this—I focused on smell. If I could anchor myself with even the smallest bit of recognition of this place, that would be the key to escape.

Parched earth, crying out for rain, that heavy, dusty reek that clogs up your nostrils with its bitterness. A hint of decay, but the dry desiccation of a mummy rather than the oozing, fleshy remains of a newly dead lump of meat. Underlying all of it was something cold, antiseptic. Just a hint of a chemical that I couldn't identify, but which promised sterility.

Another wail rose closer, and the first answered back.

What's next? Keeping my eyes firmly shut, I ran my hands along the ground. What I expected; dust, rocks, scraggly grass so dry and sharp it might cut me. I crawled, afraid to stand lest the pain bring me back to my knees, but I froze as I realized I shouldn't have been alone. Legion should've been here with me.

The chaos demon was so deeply entwined with my soul, it should've been all but impossible for them to escape me. But even as I searched, it became apparent that that was the case. How? A flash of something came back to me. Tumbling through space and time, trying to bring myself to a stop, but never able to find purchase. Finding myself back home, a young man in a world he thought he understood.

What had I been doing? Right. It was the day that the merchants were supposed to arrive with the plants I bought for my mother as a gift. She was going to add them to her garden. The only safe place she had to escape my father. My exhale was soft and abrupt. That hadn't worked out as planned.

The wails got closer, and I flinched. They had moved position, like they were boxing me in, circling their prey.

I dug deeper still, within myself, to access a power that wouldn't come. I was fragile and helpless in a hellscape.

I forced myself to keep moving. There had to be shelter somewhere, and as I stared, I could just make out more defined shapes. There was a ridge of—something—ahead, either trees or rocks. It could've been mountains.

But I was going to get there.

The terrain cut my knees, and I gritted my teeth against the pain. Warm blood rose to the surface of bruised skin, then breaking free as the sting of dirt burrowed into freshly opened wounds. The palms of my hands were in much the same shape.

The howling was chasing me, taunting me, moving ever closer. Those cries could only come from souls that had truly given up. They were doomed, and they knew it, and they railed against their circumstances so they wouldn't feel so alone. And now two such creatures were homing in on me.

I urged myself to move faster. The ridgeline was close when my fingertips brushed against something different. Something like flesh, if stone were made human.

I craned my neck upward to find a tall figure looming, the shadow bending and twisting as it swayed over me. I scurried backward, only to run into the second figure. Scrambling away, they followed, their lithe bodies almost graceful as they stalked me.

"Why do you run?"

All the air rushed out of my lungs when I heard that voice.

"We mean you no harm," said the other, and a shocked cry tore from my throat. It couldn't be them. Not in a place like this.

My voice quavered as I spoke, keeping pace with the trembling of my body. "Norah? Mother?"

"Yes, Belsioch," said my mother, a warm note in her voice. "We came to welcome you."

"No," I whispered, but they didn't seem to hear me.

"I've missed you, husband," said Norah. My eyes closed as I let myself bathe in the magickal lilt I'd missed so much. "We have much to discuss."

Gods, how I wanted that. To spend hours talking with her like I used to, wrapped in her arms as we lounged in the gardens.

But even as I thought it and wished for it to be true, this had to be a trick. "Where are we?" I asked.

"Together," said my mother, like it was the most obvious answer in the world.

"But *where*," I insisted.

"Bel," said my wife, "why does it matter? We are together again. Reunited forever."

My head shook back and forth, a constant motion as my entire body rejected that thought. "I don't believe you. Who are you, really?"

The shapes leaned down inches from my face, and the figure on the left reached for me, cold, lifeless hands caressing my cheeks. A flash of light blinded me, but that was all I needed to get the impression of the face in front of me. It might have been my mother, once. But there was so much raw agony in her eyes, the drawn gauntness and sunken cheeks speaking of long-suffered illness. No goddess of fortune could meet a fate like this.

Her nails scraped my cheeks as she straightened, and I scrambled backward as Norah reached for me. I didn't want to see her like this, but it was no use. Her hands clamped around my face. Even though I screwed my eyes closed tight, the image of her still seared itself into my brain.

She had fared far worse. She was almost skeletal, skin stretched tight over her bones, her eyes sunken and milky. Her curtain of hair had fallen out, just thin wisps of gray clinging to her scalp. Her lipless mouth twisted in a sad smile as she tilted her head to the side. "Why do you deny us?"

A keening sound wormed its way out of my chest, and I couldn't stop it. The most I could do was keep it from becoming a scream.

"Not you, can't be you," I said, desperate for those words to be truth.

Norah straightened and stood beside my mother once again, and mercifully her image faded from my mind.

"Where are we?" I demanded.

"They call it the realm of the Forsaken," my mother said, the same anguish that haunted the wailing coming through in her words.

I was familiar with the place, in legend. I shook my head so hard in denial, I almost toppled myself over. "No. Neither of you should be here. They wouldn't allow it. You don't belong here. You never belonged here."

I wept as I looked at the figure of my mother. "You are a goddess. This isn't the kind of fate the Ætherim are subject to."

"No," she agreed. "We aren't here because of our own missteps."

Norah sighed, a lonely sound. "We're here because of you."

CHAPTER FIVE

Andrus

"Do you want help collecting what you need for Arthur's bonding?" I asked Death, as the others slowly moved off elsewhere, not much left to be said.

Hadi leaned down to speak into Meg's ear and she nodded, getting up from her seat and leaving the room with him. I didn't pay much attention to where the others had gone, but when I looked around again, it was just me and Death.

Death, who was appraising me with keen interest. "Is all this helpfulness just a way to endear yourself to people, or is it genuine?"

My brow furrowed. "You think this is just an act?"

He shrugged. "Meg, I think I figured out. Gareth certainly. Remi tries to hide behind the gruffness, but his character is still plain. Felix is fae, so I don't even try to understand him or his motives. The other two are still complete mysteries." He chuckled. "That dragon is an intimidating presence."

"I would've thought I was the easiest to figure out," I said. "I'm not trying to hide anything."

"Maybe not trying," he said. "But nobody grows up with a King of Hell for a father and isn't affected in some way by it."

I froze. "Is it that obvious?"

"No. Only because I knew your father."

Shock was a mild description of what I felt. "He never mentioned you. He never missed a chance to brag about knowing powerful people."

Death's expression was hard to decipher. "I didn't say we got on well."

"Ah," I said. That made more sense. The only person my father ever really got along with was himself, and even that was contentious most of the time.

"For what it's worth, I guarantee you get exactly what you're seeing," I said. "My father was a great example of how *not* to behave."

Death said nothing, so I cut to the chase. "Did you want help? It's a genuine offer."

He nodded. "Sure. I'll take you up on that."

And he did, so here I was, heading toward a village near to his home. It had been a long time since I'd been to the Strangefells. Things changed slower in this realm, so I was curious as to what I would find.

Death's house looked as much on the outside as it did on the inside. Classic. A simple two stories, stone façade, the garden in the front of the house just as beautiful as the one in the back. A paving-stone walkway led down to a winding drive.

The walk through the woods was peaceful, and I didn't come across anything untoward. Not that I expected to, but after my last trip to the woods of another realm, I was a bit jumpy. Those spiderlike parasites still haunted my nightmares.

Cars weren't necessary here, not when teleportation was easy for even the smallest children. Once I reached the main road—more for recreation than transportation, unless you were making a show with a horse and carriage—things changed.

There were signs that the human realm had made a bigger impact here than I'd bet most people would admit. I passed a few random buildings standing on the outskirts, occupied by hearth witches, and a blacksmith more likely to supply you with weapons than reshoe your horse. And then there was an electronics repair shop.

A little farther down, things really opened up. The lane became a wide road, and the sporadic buildings became the outskirts of a town, houses lined up along each side.

Death had sent me to fetch a focus from one of the psych witches in town that had a shop right in the town square. I was assuming I could get there just from following the main road, but the more I walked, the more I wondered. Maybe I should've asked Death for directions.

The air was cool enough that keeping a brisk pace on my walk was comfortable, and it was a relief to be out of the house with a moment to myself. Granted, I wouldn't have minded one person in particular as company, but she had plenty of other things to worry about.

The town was lovely. Quiet and quaint were two words that would aptly describe it. It had grown up some from the medieval structures I was expecting after my last visit, but as I looked around, it didn't seem like a bad thing for the most part.

Modest stone houses lined streets lit with gas lamps against the twilight sky. Small gardens stood in front of each home, thick stone walls acting as low fences between. But I could see signs of the human world everywhere.

The glow of televisions—I couldn't help the curl of my lip... awful things—emanated from several front windows. Bicycles and in-line skates were tossed around on paved sidewalks, and rock 'n' roll blasted from a home up the street as smoke from a grill wafted into the air from a backyard gathering.

A small group of what appeared to be teenage magi were on the opposite side of the street, looking into glowing screens that fit in their hands. The lexicon told me they were phones, but it hurt my head just to think about it.

Modern technology was a wonder and a headache, and I hoped Meg wouldn't want to settle in a place that demanded its use once this was all over with.

A small smile crept across my face. What would that look like? Would all of us be able to live together? Just coexisting in a big house? What would the sleeping arrangements look like? It would be a shame if I lost some of that closeness with her once we were settled.

Doubt gnawed at me, not for the first time. Would we grow apart, more like roommates than mates? Each of us living separate lives, afraid to monopolize too much of Meg's time lest it cause strain between us and our brothers? Or would Meg be caught in the middle, making a schedule so she could ensure she didn't choose favorites?

She would do that, I was sure. Bend over backward to not alienate anyone, even if it broke her in the process. She needed that spontaneity, lighting up when any of us surprised her.

I didn't want to lose that. I certainly didn't want to lose her.

Shouldn't I have hit the town square by now?

I shrugged it off as paranoia. Of course I'd be expecting something to go wrong. How could I not? Up ahead I could see taller buildings, the makings of a town square if ever I'd seen one. I pushed the unease aside and continued on my journey, letting the signs of life surround me, lulling me with a hypnotizing combination. The murmur of voices, dogs barking, my footfalls on the ground, the occasional peal of laughter.

How long had I been walking now?

I had never quite gotten the hang of keeping time in the Strangefells. I honestly never even learned the basic patterns. A month of twilight, a month of complete darkness, and maybe dawn...

It didn't matter. I could still see the town square ahead of me, growing steadily closer. Death didn't give me a timeline, so maybe I could pare it down to a more leisurely stroll.

It was a nice evening, after all.

CHAPTER SIX

Gareth

Arthur wasn't the same man I knew. I couldn't fault him for losing hope and starting a life with Sasha. There were plenty of times I was ready to give up and pack it in. The Vale was the first family I'd had in a long time. They'd given me a reason to continue.

And it was there that Meg found me.

No, I didn't fault Arthur for that. It was admirable that he was sticking to his principles, not wanting to betray his wife. I was just frustrated that he couldn't see through the deceptions. That his true-mate was right in front of him and he couldn't accept it.

He couldn't even grieve Sasha and move on because she—or something that looked like her—was still walking around.

A growl ripped from my throat. This wasn't supposed to be easy, but at every turn...

The set of double doors down the hall streamed with moonlight. A run would do me good. I walked out into the courtyard, pleasantly warm and surrounded by greenery. I quickly shed my clothes and transformed.

The power that ran through the Strangefells was entirely different. My mind raced as I ran across the wide lawn toward the forest of dense, dark trees. Ferns whipped against my face as I entered the underbrush, a thick barrier to fight through as I moved deeper into the woods.

I wanted more than anything for Meg to be running alongside me, her beautiful wolf keeping pace. Things were so much simpler when it was just the two of us. Now that I was reunited with my brothers, I remembered how much we grated on each other's nerves. Too many strong personalities.

That's what family was. We fought and sniped and annoyed the ever-loving-fuck out of each other, but there was nobody I'd rather face this challenge with. I'd trust them with my life, and more importantly, with Meg's life, no matter how we disagreed.

Somewhere ahead, I heard water gurgling in a rushing torrent and I headed for it, tongue sticky with thirst. I broke out of the trees onto a muddy bank strewn and slippery with leaves. My paws dug into the mud to find purchase as I dipped my head to drink.

The cool water elicited a sigh, and I took the chance to stop and look around. The full moons hung heavy overhead. I hadn't noticed it before, but some trees were glowing with an indigo light, shedding small pools of illumination throughout the densely packed forest.

I had yet to run across any other beasties that roamed territory like this, and I realized with an uneasy shudder that I wasn't an apex predator in this place. It was foolish not to have been more careful, leaving such an obvious trail and making so much noise.

Now that I thought about it, I couldn't recall how far I'd run, either. I should head back.

The brief scent of musk tickled my nose, and my hunting instinct kicked into overdrive. I licked my lips as the enticing aroma of deer wafted toward me, but I shook it off. Dragging a dead deer carcass back to Death's house wouldn't win me any esteem. He'd be more likely to kick me out for getting deer blood on his floors, although I still didn't fear his reactions as much as I feared Farah's.

I smiled, my wolfish mouth twisting unnaturally. Meg was lucky to have had someone like the old sphinx looking out for her.

Dense foliage seemed to drag me backward as I turned from all thoughts of bringing down the deer and headed back. Then a stronger scent carried toward me. Bear.

My favorite thing to hunt.

Maybe I could afford just a little longer. I didn't have to kill it, just tracking it would be enough to keep my wolf sated.

A quick jump across the river and I took off after it, keeping low to the ground, scenting nonstop. My mouth salivated, and my determination not to kill was quickly fading.

Control was for those who didn't know what to do with their power. I was an alpha. That alone demanded respect. I was tired of keeping my wolf in check. Tiptoeing around Meg as I tried to be a team player. A snarl broke the darkness, and I realized it was mine.

I didn't want to share. Shouldn't have to. She was *mine*.

It had taken everything I had in me not to attack Hadi as he'd wrapped his tail around her, trying to claim her for himself.

It was unlikely I'd be able to best him in a fight, but dammit if I didn't want to try.

Meg was mine first. *Mine!* None of the others loved her as much as I did. They couldn't. We found each other first. She came to me first. We'd been on this journey together since the beginning.

I was running now, full tilt toward the scent of the bear. It was close. And I would relish the feel of its blood gushing into my mouth as I ripped out its throat. I would gorge myself on the meat, taking as much as I wanted because I wouldn't *have* to share.

Breaking through into a clearing, the scent was all around me. It had to be right here. I circled around the edges, but all roads led to this spot. It should be here.

A frustrated howl tore from my throat, and it felt liberating to let go of all my rage and frustration and anger. To not have to keep it bottled up. Gods forbid that somebody misinterpret my actions and get their feelings hurt. We all have our weaknesses, drawbacks, shortcomings, vices. They know me, and they know my personality. It was unreasonable of them to expect me to play fair. To demand I be something I'm not.

Because I won't share. Meg is mine, and I'll show them all what that means, even Hadi.

The crack of twigs to the left stopped me, and I looked back to see a shape emerging from the shadow of the trees. Feral eyes met mine, wild with hunger, and I bared my teeth in a snarl. The creature didn't seem very big. Maybe it would back down quickly.

The shape stepped into the moonlight.

CHAPTER SEVEN

Meg

When Hadi took my hand and led me out of the room, butterflies went crazy in my stomach. There was just something about him I couldn't figure out. An aura that surrounded him. He was very private, which wasn't a bad thing, but all the rest of my men were relatively open books, even Remi, despite what he wanted to think.

But Hadi kept everything close to the vest. He only spoke when he needed to. Emotions were carefully curated. He was the only dragon I'd ever met, to my knowledge, so I wasn't sure if this was a trait all dragons shared, or if it was just how he was.

And for all my nerves, I was drawn to him. Every molecule of my being wanted to be near him, and that made me uncomfortable. I couldn't imagine he was holding some kind of magick over me, besides the usual fiery attraction that I'd felt with my mates after the initial danger surrounding our meeting had passed.

But maybe this was just a sign that this part of the journey was almost complete. All my mates were here with me. Things were still complicated with Arthur, but we'd figure it out. And even if he didn't become my mate in the traditional sense, he was still a part of this family.

Just thinking about that calmed my nerves. Despite all the curveballs we'd been thrown, we were exactly where we needed to be. Of that, I was sure.

Hadi still hadn't spoken a word as he led me through the house toward the double doors of the back garden. "How are you finding your way around so easily?" I asked.

He glanced at me, eyebrow raised. "What do you mean?"

I shivered as the liquid gold of his voice seeped into me. "It just seems like you know your way around the house, but I'm pretty sure you've never been here before."

A grin pulled at his mouth. "No, I haven't. I smelled fresh air, so I followed."

I nodded. That made sense, but it still surprised me. I thought my senses were keen, but I hadn't noticed any such thing. Or maybe I just wasn't paying attention. He was definitely a man who noticed the smallest details.

We walked out into the back garden, and I let myself soak it in for a minute, while he seemed to do the same. Tall hedges and garden walls kept the air close, so the temperature was comfortable. The pale colors of the flowers glowed in the twilight, and I gravitated to a patch of jasmine, inhaling the exotic scent.

"Lovely," said Hadi.

I turned to see what he was looking at, and found him looking squarely at me, his eyes seeking, searching for depths I would be happy to let him explore.

What was I doing? I shook my head, stopping myself short before I walked over to him. There had to be something. This was not normal behavior for me.

"Is something wrong?" he asked, concerned.

I planted my feet firmly to fight the pull that was drawing me to him. "Are you enchanting me somehow?"

His head cocked to the side. "No." He took a step closer. "Why do you ask?"

My cheeks felt hot. Saying it out loud was far more embarrassing. Maybe it was just all in my head. Before I could respond, he smiled, warm and genuine, and my heart did a small tap dance before settling back into its normal rhythm.

"That, right there. How are you affecting me like this?" I demanded, letting my irritation cover my embarrassment.

Mirth filled his eyes, an honest-to-gods sparkle, and he laughed. I could've wrapped myself up in that laugh and stayed there, cozy and secure, for the rest of eternity. I shook it off again, more vigorously this time, and crossed my arms. "Stop that," I said, glaring at him.

His shoulders were shaking as he fought to stifle his laughter. "My apologies," he said, bowing his head. "I take it you aren't used to keeping company with dragons?"

"No." One-syllable words were all I was capable of at the moment.

"May I?" Hadi asked, holding out his hand.

I looked at it suspiciously. "Why?"

"Dragons... shed... a lot of pheromones and power. You are already hyper attuned to these things. That, combined with the fact that we are soon to be mated"—his tongue lingered on the word and it did all sorts of unspeakable things to me—"might be overwhelming you." He took another step closer. "I'm only going to help level you out."

Still unsure of what to think, I nodded. He didn't want to hurt me, so if it could help, what did it hurt to try?

Hadi's hand was warm as he pressed it against my chest. An electric sensation spread across my skin, head to toe, until my entire body was buzzing. Being this close to him was indeed overwhelming, and my breath came in short pants. Warmth spread through my core, and I watched his pupils dilate as he sensed a different kind of prey. My thoughts became more jumbled than they had been.

Lightheadedness took over, and I swayed on my feet, Hadi's other hand gripping my arm to keep me from—my teeth clenched at the thought—swooning. Every sensation cranked up to a thousand, and then it was done. It all swirled away, water down a drain, and I felt like myself again. I smiled and placed my hands on Hadi's face, to prove to myself that I wouldn't lose my mind and throw myself at him. "Thank you," I said.

"My pleasure." He tilted my chin upward and placed a light kiss on my lips. Warmth spread through me again, but nothing I couldn't control. He leaned in and spoke, breath light on the shell of my ear. "I look forward to bringing you to new heights, now that it's on your terms."

My gods, it took all the willpower I had not to call everybody together and get to the mating right then. "Is there something you wanted to speak to me about?" I asked, taking a firm step back. He had to have brought me out here for some reason other than testing my ability to resist him.

"Nothing in particular," he admitted. "I wanted to get to know you a little better. We haven't had much time to talk."

That was an understatement. "Only if I get to ask you questions too."

"Of course." He guided us to a bench, and we made ourselves comfortable. I was grateful that most of the places we ended up so far had such beautiful, extensive gardens. I couldn't imagine there would be much by way of nature and greenery to enjoy once we got to the lower realms of hell.

We sat there for hours, talking and just enjoying each other's company. The conversation never turned very serious, sticking mostly to surface level "getting to know you" type questions, which was nice. Having to delve deep and scrape the bottom of my soul daily was exhausting.

It wasn't until my belly growled that I realized how long we'd been sitting there.

"Thank goodness," he said, placing a hand on his abdomen. "Our stomachs are in agreement."

"We should fix that," I said, getting to my feet. "I wonder what Death keeps his kitchen stocked with?"

Turns out it was pretty average fair, and we weren't the first ones to gravitate there. Arthur was standing at the cooktop and he offered me a smile when we entered. "What are you making? It smells incredible."

"Just something I've been throwing together," he said.

I leaned closer over the pot, simmering with vegetables and chunks of meat, along with the heavenly aroma coming from the oven. "Are you making bread from scratch?" I asked, mouth already watering.

"Not quite. He had a popover tin, so I made Yorkshire puddings," said Arthur.

Another phrase I never thought I'd hear. Death had a popover tin in his kitchen.

Arthur finally relaxed as we ate, all gathered around the central table, minus Gareth, Andrus and Felix. Death had joined us as well, tucking in with obvious enjoyment of the meal.

"Doesn't anybody ever feed you?" I asked him.

"I don't actually have to eat," said Death.

"But you enjoy food," I said.

"I'm a busy shepherd, not a lot of time to waste on things I don't need." He gave me a simpering smile. "Anyway, once Andrus gets back with that focus, we can begin with the bonding," said Death. He looked at the watch on his wrist. "Although he probably should've been back by now. He must've gotten distracted."

"I can't say I've ever been to a village in the Strangefells," I said after swallowing a big mouthful of stew. "It was just a pass-through point, between the underworld and the human realm for me. I've been to a few of the bigger cities."

Death shrugged. "They all function pretty much the same. Only difference is, you're more likely to get bitten by a werewolf toddler than somebody's stray dog."

I snorted. "Good to know. I'll keep an eye out for that."

"You'll be able to send a call to the others, won't you?" Death continued. "I have no idea where Gareth and Felix have gotten off to."

"When did Felix leave?" Remi asked. "I was talking to him not too long before we sat down for the meal."

"He might be making it a point to wait until I leave before he grabs some food," said Arthur.

Remi pulled a face. "He's upset, but not necessarily at you. You know how he hates drama when he's not the cause of it. I don't think he would avoid you, especially when there's food on the table."

Something about that wasn't sitting right. "Maybe I should just reach out to them, make sure everyone's okay," I said, excusing myself from the table after finishing the last bites of Yorkshire pudding. "The meal was delicious, thank you."

Arthur smiled. "Anytime."

I went back to my room and settled into the chaise lounge in the corner. It had a very distinctive Victorian-era vibe, which, the more I encountered this furniture throughout Death's home, I realized meant it was going to be uncomfortable.

I focused on the three men's signatures. I could track them through time, but trying to communicate directly took a different finesse.

My impressions of them were faded. Distance shouldn't matter, and Andrus was only supposed to be going into town. Gareth went to clear his head, last I knew. He could go a long way on a run, but I couldn't imagine he would allow himself to get that far, not when he knew there were things we needed to do.

Didn't Remi say that Felix must've just left?

I tried to settle my nerves, that inkling of fear spreading. This was supposed to be a safe place. Death would have warned us of anything out of the ordinary, right?

With a few deep, calming breaths, I tried again, putting out a bit more of my power. They felt just out of reach, no matter how many times I tried, or how many ways. It reminded me of being in a dream, where you're chasing somebody and they're always one step ahead of you, disappearing around a corner right before you get there.

Shit.

CHAPTER EIGHT

Felix

"I think Arthur is making food if you want to join?" Remi said, the set of his face implying he was unsure how I would react.

"I'll join you later," I said, not sure if I actually would. It was still a bit too much to handle to be around Arthur right now. "I was going to go exploring, check out what else Death is hiding around his house. I'm sure she has a stash of the good liquor that's not in the cabinet with the rest of it," I joked, pulling my usual deflection-by-way-of-comedy card. Remi knew I was bullshitting, but he shrugged it off and walked away.

There was no way in hell I was going to go snooping. Not here. Death's secrets were her own.

Maybe she had a gym somewhere. I was about ready to crawl out of my skin with restlessness. Now that we were on the verge of finishing this, I just wanted to get it over with.

An odd shade of golden light was emanating from a doorway up ahead. It was cracked open, and the light seemed to intensify as I got nearer to it. A gentle push was all it took, and the door swung wide. I'm not sure what I was expecting to see, but open woodland would've been at the bottom of that list.

"This seems like a trap," I said, nodding my head. I turned to walk away. This was one of those secrets that Death was going to keep all to herself.

A sharp tug brought me up short. I jerked away from it, but its grip tightened and with a jerk that bottomed out my stomach, I went flying backward through the door. The light surrounded me as I heard the door slam shut.

I opened my eyes to dim twilight, a far cry from the golden glimmer that brought me here. I was laying at the mouth of a cave, in the middle of deep woods. A few crickets chirped in a sad attempt to find each other. A crow squawked, but received no answer. Other than that, it was stillness.

I blew out a breath. "Well," I said, getting to my feet, "let's see what fresh hell is in store for us today."

Meg was just out of reach when I tapped into our bond. The others were equally unreachable. I sucked my teeth. Very thorough. Cut me off from everyone, drop me in the middle of nowhere, and leave me to my own devices.

I couldn't sense any threat, so I was eighty-five percent sure that this was a trick, not a trap in someone's deadly game. And if this was a trap, I was insulted that they thought a little isolation would be enough to do me in.

My hair hung loose around my shoulders, but that wouldn't do for adventuring, now would it? I pulled an elastic out of my pocket—I was still on the fence whether I liked them better than the leather ties I was used to—and did a quick braid.

The darkness of the cave was all-encompassing. Even though my people had evolved from the darkness itself, just as able to thrive underground as above it, this elf had no desire to go into the yawning abyss. At the very least because I hated spiders, and that cave reeked of them.

A new perspective was needed.

Tall birch were dotted among the oak and ash. I leaped to grab hold of the lowest hanging branch and hauled myself into the tree, pushing through the leaves to the tallest branch that could support my weight.

The sea of trees that surrounded me seemed unbroken until I spotted a spire in the distance. A clock tower. Perhaps I was still near Death's house after all. The more I looked at it, the more I could discern a wider, open space around it where the lower buildings must've been, and now that I knew what pattern to look for, there were straight lines indicating streets cutting through the trees.

That settled it then. I made my way back to the ground, and set off at a brisk pace, heading for that clock tower and already planning my vengeance on whoever had orchestrated this impromptu hike. Hilarious, trying to prank the prankster.

Oh, yes, revenge would be sweet.

Which one of my brothers could've done this? And why? I'd pulled a lot of pranks over the years, but you'd think two thousand years was enough of a cooling-off period that they would've gotten over it.

I ticked off my past pranks on my fingers as I remembered them.

Switching the terrain maps Andrus was going to march his troops over. Planting a stolen necklace from Macedonian royalty on Gareth. Spreading a rumor about Hadi plotting a coup against his own dragon king. Having Remi fly into a storm on a rescue mission for a person who didn't exist. Convincing Arthur that the Seelie queen had removed his protections and taken back his power, so he had to go into hiding.

A frown sagged on my face. In retrospect, I was an asshole. All those pranks could've ended badly, and many of them almost did. Hadi's head was on the chopping block before I was able to convince them it was all a hoax. Andrus had wound up walking right into the enemy camp. He still secured a victory, but more people were lost than should've been.

I'd tried to laugh it off. All fun and games. The people that died signed up for it. They knew what might await them in battle.

My steps hitched. Why had I ever found amusement in that? What was I trying to achieve? To prove? Other than that, I was a liability. Why had they put up with it? The Titans should've banished me the first time I almost got one of us killed.

The more I thought about it, the sicker I felt. I had put my friends, my brothers, the men I made a vow to give my life for, that I would trust with my own, in danger for nothing other than a cheap thrill that must've filled some kind of hole within myself. But nothing ever lasted, because I kept doing it.

They had every right to be angry at me, to hold a grudge, and exact their own kind of vengeance. Which, given the trespasses that might've warranted this prank, seemed out of balance. Dropping me in the middle of a forest and giving me plenty of time to think about what I'd done might be something that Andrus would've done, maybe even Hadi. But I hadn't really shown that I'd changed much, so why would they have any reason to believe I would use this time for introspection?

Maybe this wasn't just a prank after all.

How long had I been walking? I climbed another tree, finding the clock tower still in the distance, but I wasn't any closer to it. I knew I'd been walking for at least an hour or two. Something was wrong here. I tried to reach out through the bond again, but was denied.

That first hit of panic struck me out of the blue as all the pieces of the puzzle came together. I was cut off from my mate and my brothers. I was isolated in the wilderness. And it was becoming increasingly clear that there was no way out.

I was definitely in trouble.

CHAPTER NINE

Meg

I jumped to my feet and headed for the dining room, a cold determination burning away the worry. There was no point in it. Fuck all this shit.

Remi was already on his feet when I walked in the room, having felt my emotions through the bond.

"What's wrong?" he asked.

"I tried to contact them, but something is keeping them away. I can sense them, but they're on the very edge of my awareness and I can't get any closer." I looked at Death. "Any idea as to what might be causing it?"

His face was set in a severe frown. "No." He rubbed his chin. "Nothing should be able to do that anywhere near my house. This is my territory. Everyone knows it."

"But for argument's sake, let's say they don't care," said Remi.

Death didn't even chastise him for it. "I still would've felt a strange magick being worked here. There's nothing."

"Are there any chaos demons that specialize in hiding like that?" I asked.

Death's lips pursed while he thought. "There are only a handful that I've had any encounters with, and it feels like they've all come after you already." He lapsed into silence that stretched out for so long I had to double check that time was still moving like it should.

We were staring at him intently when his head popped back up. He smiled when I yelped and jumped back. "Had to run through the ol' mental encyclopedia. It was pretty dusty." He made a "yikes" face. "Twixt is probably the one we're looking for."

"What kind of name is that?" asked Remi. "I don't recognize it."

Death snorted. "His original name is long gone. That seems to be a rough translation of what people have settled for."

"Like betwixt?" I asked, already not liking where this was going.

"Just like that." Death sat back in his chair. "Twixt is the chaos demon that specializes in liminal spaces. He can move between them just as easily as manipulate them." He rubbed at his temples. "These pricks are starting to get on my nerves." He stood and made a big show of stretching. "Let's go, then. He's trespassed, and he needs to pay the price for it."

"You're coming with us?" I asked.

"Oh, yes," he said, a dangerous glint in his eye. "He should've known better than to come this close to my home."

"What if it isn't just Twixt?" Arthur asked. "What if it isn't Twixt at all?"

Death looked at him scathingly. The two of them had been in an unspoken stalemate since Arthur was brought back. "You are all catnip for chaos demons. Let's assume the worst here."

"Let's walk and talk," I said, not wanting to give Twixt any more time to do whatever he was planning.

Once we got outside and hit the main road, Remi looked at me. "Should we split up?"

I shook my head vehemently. "Hell no. That's what started this mess in the first place. They all went off alone."

"It will be a lot easier to find them," said Hadi.

"Your entire perspective on life is going to be changed when you start watching horror movies," said Death, tone droll.

Hadi looked at me for an explanation and I grinned despite the situation. "You never split up, unless you have a death wish." Death made a noise and I rolled my eyes. "No pun intended."

"This is the only situation you'll ever be in where that *is* a pun," he said, annoyed that he had to battle back a smile.

I made a quick decision. "We go after Andrus first. Together."

Death pointed. "Town is this way."

We headed off down the lane. "What else do you know about Twixt's magick?" I asked. "Any idea how he could be trapping them like he is?"

Death shook his head. "Not really. The one time I had any dealings with him at all was largely through word of mouth. It was around the time of the Crusades. A cadre of knights had been sent to hunt him down. Only one of the knights reappeared, with a story of being trapped in an underground tunnel. The exit was always just out of reach."

"That sounds like a psychological trap," Arthur said. "Not something physical."

I cocked my head. "Like they might be trapped somewhere together? In an illusion?" I knew a thing or two about that. Memories of Morpheus and Hypnos flooded back. It had been so real as they'd crushed my bones and made me beg for mercy. When they made me think that Gareth had betrayed me.

"Just a thought," he said, helpless. "We might waste time looking far and wide or between dimensions and they could be napping under a tree together."

"At least let me fly overhead," said Remi. "I'll stay within sight at all times. Promise."

I looked at Death, who nodded. "It should be okay."

The idea still seemed risky, but the reality was that "okay" was as good as we were going to get.

"Go," I said, and Remi unfurled his wings and took to the sky with a rush of air.

"Is everybody alright with jump-stepping?" I asked, needing this to go faster.

Nods all around and we tapped into the magick that most humans associated automatically with supernatural beings. The ability to move faster than the eye could see. The world blurred around us, but my companions were still in focus, their speed matching mine.

About time I got to test out my speed, said Remi through the bond. I felt his exhilaration as his wings powered through the air, pushing faster.

As we ran, I tried to think of what the demon's purpose was. Was he just trying to fuck with us? What purpose would it serve to separate us in some kind of endless loop? It seemed very benign for a chaos demon. You would think the first order of business upon getting any of us alone would be to try to kill us. That's what would really serve their endgame, wouldn't it?

What was I missing? And was there any significance to the fact that the three men that were lured away were my first three mates? That felt significant, but I didn't know why.

I reached out to Andrus's signature again, hoping something would've changed. He still felt distant, but there was a shaky quality to the barrier. Because we were getting closer?

I narrowly avoided blurry shapes appearing in the middle of the road, small squares of light in their hands. The girls yelled curses after us as we passed, the equivalent of a car cutting them off in the bike lane. But it gave me an idea. They'd had phones, which ping locations. Not in the Strangefells as there are no satellites—it was this whole huge thing to get them to work here—but what if... I shoved my power through the bond. It hit the barrier and ricocheted back, the resulting waves giving me a direction and damaging that invisible wall in the process.

"This way!" I called, turning to a side street. Andrus already felt closer. I did it again, and again, battering the wall with power until I sensed it was ready to fall. With one more burst, it came shattering down and the vampire lit up like a beacon.

In seconds, we were there, appearing in front of him so suddenly that he leaped back, ready to defend himself. When he realized it was us, he just looked confused.

"What are you doing here?" He looked at Death. "I haven't been to the shop yet. I guess I got distracted."

I shook my head. "No. We think there's another chaos demon messing with us."

His face fell. "I knew something felt off." He cursed. "I should've listened to my gut." His anger sizzled through the bond, but it was anger at himself, not the demon.

I hugged him as Remi landed with us. "Gareth and Felix are in danger too." I looked around at all of them. "I'm afraid we're missing something. It was too easy to find Andrus. Is this a distraction for something else?"

"We don't even know where to start looking for the others, do we?" Arthur asked.

"Actually," I said, repeating my new trick. "Of course. They're both in the woods, one on the east side, one on the west." I gestured around. Beside the wide street and cozy rows of houses that made up the bulk of this town, it was nothing but woods as far as the eye could see.

"Now we should split up," Death said, looking grim. "If either one of them is in real danger, we can't waste any time."

"Teams of three?" I suggested.

"Pffft," said Death, waving his hand. "Catnip, remember? I'll be better off without you." He grinned. "You all stick together. I'll go after Felix." He paused. "If either one of them is in more trouble right now, my bet's on Gareth."

My breath hitched as Death confirmed my own suspicions. Gareth was my first mate. I still didn't know why, but it seemed too significant.

Death nodded and made to walk away, but I stopped him. "How will you know where to look? I was kind of... echolocating them."

"Dear, this is my territory. I have my ways. Now hurry," he said, waving us off. "Call out if you find him, and I'll do the same."

Death disappeared.

I turned to Hadi. "Can you shift and carry me with you?"

His lips parted in surprise. "Yes."

"What are you planning?" Remi asked.

"I do the same thing that I did to find Andrus," I said. "Latch onto Gareth's signature and smash it with power until it breaks whatever barrier is surrounding him. Andrus was easy to find because he was in a straight line ahead of us, but out there..."

"Isn't this the same as splitting up?" Remi asked. "We won't have a line of sight to each other. Not as thick as those trees are."

"There will be three of us on the ground, and two in the air," said Arthur, matter-of-factly. "We won't actually be alone."

"Sounds like a plan," said Andrus, and Remi nodded reluctantly.

Hadi stepped away and shed his clothing. I tried not to stare, but it was a feast for the eyes. When he began to shift, my mouth dropped open in amazement. Within seconds, a beautiful opalescent dragon was standing in the middle of the road, so massive that he would've taken out the houses on other side of him if he'd opened his wings. Spiked ridges ran down his back and tail, and over the crown of his head, three in total. His tail curled as he held out a giant, clawed hand, almost as wide as I was tall.

Suddenly, I regretted this decision. He sensed my discomfort, and a low rumble bubbled up his chest. Was he laughing?

I narrowed my eyes and stepped forward, but flinched back at the last second as Hadi's hand reached for me. The laughter sounded again and he reached out his long neck, snatching me up quickly but carefully in his teeth, and took off running down the street to get clearance. It was alarming how fast he could move on the ground, but that was nothing compared to when he snapped open his gargantuan wings and took to the sky. The ground hurtled away from us so fast my stomach rolled, and I vomited.

We were already so high up I couldn't see the ground clearly, but I hoped that the other three had gotten out of the way.

Hadi laughed again and beat his wings as he soared higher.

"Okay, that should be good enough!" I called, hoping he could hear me over the rushing of wind. Now that I was used to communicating mentally with my mates, having to shout seemed like the biggest inconvenience in the world.

I had a death grip on his claw as I tried not to look down.

Really great time to remember how much you hate heights, Meg.

He leveled out. Hadi was so large and fast that we could easily circle over the woods and cover plenty of ground in a hurry, even as massive as the grounds were. I sent out the locating blast, but there was more resistance with Gareth's barrier, a steel plate compared to the chicken wire that was around Andrus. That only confirmed my fears. He was being targeted, and the demon wanted to keep us from finding him as long as possible.

I battered against it with all the force I could summon, sending a message to my mates while guiding Hadi in the right direction with fumbling hand signals. We were close.

I spotted a clearing up ahead. "There! Can you put me down over there?" I shouted.

Hadi dove and my arms wrapped around one of his giant fingers, holding on for dear life. He canted his wings to slow his descent and got as low as he could before dropping me. I rolled and transformed into my wolf simultaneously, my mates and Arthur bursting out of the woods right behind as they fell into step alongside me.

Hadi roared and kept circling overhead.

Remi, join Hadi and tell him where we are.

The gargoyle did as I asked. I pulled power from my mates and hammered the barrier. It wrenched apart and shattered with an audible noise that boomed through the woods.

Gareth!

No answer. I spurred my pace.

"Gareth!" Andrus called.

I sent a message out to Death, hoping he would get it, just as we burst onto the riverbank and I saw the flash of a knife.

Chapter Ten

Gareth

Sasha came lurching out of the trees, but she was barely holding onto her stolen mask. She had been less horrifying as a construct. Veins were standing out starkly on her face, throbbing, inky-black in color, like her blood had turned to sludge.

All my anger evaporated as my head cleared. Had I been under some kind of spell?

A line of yellowish drool fell from her mouth and her face looked like she smashed it into something multiple times, her teeth bloodied and broken.

Her limbs looked thinner, ganglier, with far too many joints.

"Stop," she snarled, taking a step forward.

Then her voice changed, not as deep. "I don't want to be here. It's too risky," she said, muttering in a mad spitting flurry. "He wants me to hurt you. It needs to be done."

He *who*?

Sasha stepped closer and I snapped at her, but she wasn't deterred.

"I tried to walk away, but he wouldn't let me. He says I need to finish this. I need to do what I was supposed to do. Meg was nice to me. She gave me a chance. She didn't cast me out with all of her suspicions."

I shifted back into my human form.

"And why are you really here?" I asked.

"Interference," she said, twitching and scratching at her hair which came out in clumps. "Casting doubt."

I took no joy in being right about that. "Who's ordering you to do all this?"

"He is," she said, her eyes fixed on her hands. I looked around quickly, just in case we weren't alone anymore, but there was nobody near.

"Who's he?" I asked again.

She just twitched and spasmed in response, muttering under her breath. "He is, he is, he is…"

"Were you ever Sasha? Or are you just wearing her skin?"

Her head snapped up and a grin spread ear to ear, the voice deepening. "She was here. But I cast her out. She wasn't necessary."

Then the grin disappeared, and demeanor returned to the nervous, twitching woman.

"Needed my face, needed my face…" She dug her fingernails into her cheeks. "Tried to get away. Wanted to spare him."

"Arthur?" I guessed.

She nodded. "Not his fault, wanted to spare him. Tried to get away. I left him. Left all of you. Tried to get away."

I took a step forward as her fingernails shredded into her cheeks, but the sudden movement made her stop. Her hand whipped to the small her back and reappeared, holding a knife. The thin silver blade shone with a dangerous glint. It was real silver. She came prepared to do damage.

"Put the knife down. We're just talking," I said, trying to sound soothing.

"No more talking," she hissed, spittle flying from her mouth. "This ends. Ends now." A brief moment of ecstasy flashed across her face. "Then I can go home."

The full extent of her possession became clear when she lunged at me faster than I could follow. I barely evaded the blade, shifting back into my wolf. I'd always fought better on four legs.

I ducked under her next swing, tearing into her side with my teeth. She screeched and stumbled backward, kicking at me and catching me in the face. I shook it off and lunged again, almost reaching her throat, but she threw up her arm to block me the last second, following with a knife swing that caught me across the chest.

The burn of the silver was immediate, my fur singed and sizzling. The warning prickling of fire melted through my veins, and it wouldn't take long before my blood was so poisoned I couldn't move.

I ran, trying to put distance between me and the slavering creature that used to be Sasha.

Gareth!

My momentary distraction allowed Sasha to catch me and cut across the side of my face as I turned to find the voice that called me. Was that Meg?

I bucked her off and ran again, finding my way to the river just as my back legs gave out. I twisted aside avoiding the leap that would've landed Sasha right on top of me. The knife plunged deep into the mud and she fought to get it free.

"Gareth!" another voice called. Andrus?

Sasha stood, a triumphant smile on her face. "They won't get to you in time. No time. Dead."

I launched myself at her. Meg and the others were getting closer, I just had to—

My yelp was loud as a stab landed between my ribs. Sasha, that manic glint in her eye, pulled the blade back and allowed me to get a good look at it, coated with my blood.

She stabbed me again in the gut and I pushed past the pain, clamping my teeth around her arm and biting down hard. The bones snapped between my jaws and she howled, punching at me with her other hand. She struggled to get free, but I wasn't giving her another chance to stab me.

We fought. Andrus and Meg led the pack as they burst onto the riverbank. Sasha snarled, grabbing the knife with her free hand and plunged it into my chest.

The breath whooshed out of my lungs, and I lost my balance, slipping off the edge of the bank into the river, taking Sasha with me as my teeth tightened around her arm.

"Gareth!" Andrus shouted.

The water was carrying us away too fast. Meg ran after us, but the banks were too slippery to get traction. She ducked into the woods, but the dense pack of the foliage slowed her down. Her frustrated howl rushed after us across the water.

Remi, follow the river, she called through the bond.

The rush of wings broke through the trees and through vision going hazy at the edges, I saw the gargoyle launch into action, his form just a darker shadow in the twilight sky. Far overhead, a dragon wheeled, its silhouette stark against the full moon.

I would've laughed if I wasn't too busy fighting to keep my head above water. For all his power, the dragon was too big to fit between the trees without bringing them all down and putting us at further risk.

My hold on Sasha loosened as my bleeding became too severe. The blackness at the edge of my vision crept closer and it was all I could do to stay conscious.

Sasha broke away and swam toward shore, but I couldn't find the strength. The world went dark and I felt the water close around my head just as two hands yanked me upward and everything came back into focus as pain tore through me.

"Sorry," Remi said, heading quickly for dry ground. He set me gently down at the same time Sasha scrambled onto shore. A silver blur tore from the woods and crashed into her, taking the woman down in a blink. Meg pinned her to the ground, jaws around her throat, a vicious growl and shake making Sasha go still.

Andrus hurried over to me and lay his hands on my wounds. "This looks bad," he murmured, poking around. "Silver?" he asked.

My transition back was painful and slow as my body fought against the effects of the poison in my blood. When I'd regained my human form, I nodded, unable to speak around shallow breaths. I craned my neck toward Meg. Her lupine eyes flashed to me before she shook Sasha again, drawing blood from punctures in the woman's neck.

"Sasha!" Arthur shouted. "Meg, what are you doing?"

I growled and spat through gritted teeth. "She attacked me!"

Arthur noticed me lying there for the first time and did a double take, glancing back and forth between me and Sasha. "She did that?" he asked, shaking his head.

Andrus let out a frustrated hiss. "We saw her do it, Arthur. She was stabbing him when we found them. She's not your wife!"

"If she is, they've got other issues besides just this," Remi muttered.

"Arthur," Sasha whimpered, grimacing when Meg clamped down harder on her throat. "Arthur, please."

"Don't listen to her!" Andrus shouted.

Remi grabbed Arthur's arm. "Listen to them," he said. "She's got blood on her hands. This isn't Sasha. Not anymore."

Arthur was staring at the scene before him, frozen and unable to comprehend. "How—"

A wave of dizziness turned my vision gray and I felt myself tip back before Andrus caught me.

"Where's Hadi?" he shouted.

"I'm here." Hadi ran up the bank from wherever he'd found room to shift, pausing only briefly as he took in the scene around him. He hurried to my side and Andrus filled him in before Hadi darted off into the woods.

I could feel the silver flowing through my blood, the poison working its way deeper, helped along by each painful beat of my heart.

It was getting harder to maintain focus. Unconsciousness took me again and when I came to the arguing was reaching a new pitch. Meg had transformed back, still pinning Sasha with a clawed stone hand clamped around her throat, fangs bared.

Hadi returned, a bundle of a wild herb in his hands. He chewed the green stalks that smelled like garlic and spat out the resulting paste, stuffing it into my wounds. I focused solely on Meg to take my mind off the process and the warm gloop being pressed into my body.

She was breathtaking. My warrior was back, that same fire I saw when she'd taken up arms to protect the Vale against the attacking humans, not hesitating to take an axe to a man's neck to protect those she loved. The bond was still clear enough through my haze that I could feel how badly she wanted vengeance. But she was also very keen to protect Arthur.

She wanted to save him from himself and this mimic of Sasha.

"Arthur, don't come any closer," she said, her eyes shining bright violet as she stared down at the woman squirming to get free from her grip.

Hadi breathed a light fire on my wounds to seal them and my concentration broke as the pain finally got to me. It wasn't hot enough to blister my skin, but it made me keenly aware of how cold the rest of my body was. Once the task was done, my body responded immediately. The burning in my veins slowed.

"Don't let her hurt me," said Sasha, reaching her hand toward Arthur. "I trusted you, Meg. I thought we were friends."

Meg's eyes narrowed, but she said nothing.

"I remember now," she continued. "The castle. Meeting you as you were running laundry for Helga."

"That's convenient," said Meg, ice in her voice.

Arthur took another step forward.

"No!" Meg snarled at him. He stopped in his tracks, shocked. Her ferocity took all of us aback; even Hadi's eyes widened in surprise which was as much telegraphing as he ever did of his emotions.

"Arthur," Sasha cried. "Please. I'm sorry I walked away, I wasn't thinking."

Power was building around Meg. Now that we were in the Strangefells, there was no barrier to her drawing of power. It danced around her, answering her call as she made a fist. It glowed with energy, purple and indigo light flashing between her fingers.

"Arthur!" The words were barely out of Sasha's mouth when two things happened simultaneously. Arthur rushed forward and Meg plunged her fist into Sasha's chest.

A brilliant flash of light blinded me, and a shock wave knocked everyone standing to the ground. A good thing for Arthur, his charge forward stopped short as the ground surrounding the two women was obliterated, exploding outward and around them right before it collapsed.

"Meg!" I shouted, struggling to get up.

But Hadi and Remi were already sprinting toward the sinkhole and diving in, Hadi sticking with his half-human form as he dove, unfurling his wings just a second after Remi as they disappeared.

CHAPTER ELEVEN

Meg

It was the gleam in Sasha's eyes that made up my mind. The cruel twist of her mouth as she called out for help. If there had been any doubt that this was a mimic, it was gone now.

The power swelled around me faster than I anticipated and I may have gotten a bit... carried away. Her call for Arthur pushed me past all semblance of control as indignation burned me. How dare this thing play on his emotions like that? On all our emotions.

The anger drove a huge burst of power through me, and I didn't realize until my fist was plunging into her chest that I might've made a miscalculation.

Her face contorted, mouth opening in a silent shriek as the magick tore her apart from the inside out. My intent was to separate her from the chaos demon, but that's certainly not what happened.

The ground around us exploded in a shower of mud and rocks and the firm land underneath us gave way. We were falling, my fist still stuck in the imposter's chest.

Gareth's voice called out my name, but the surface already seemed so far above us. How deep was this hole?

Shadows passed over us, backlit by the moons and then Remi and Hadi were there.

Remi scooped me up in his arms and Hadi pulled Sasha away with a wrenching tug. The gargoyle kicked off the wall and soared back to the surface, holding me tightly to his chest.

Arthur peered over the edge of the hole as we got closer, as did Gareth and Andrus, but they were on one side of the hole while Arthur sat alone on the other.

Remi landed gently on solid ground, and Hadi appeared moments later, dragging Sasha by one arm. She was unconscious, her body hanging limp in his grasp. He threw her down where she landed in a heap on the muddy bank.

The dragon transformed back into his fully human form and stood guard over the unconscious woman. As she lay there, she looked completely helpless, no sign of the demon within her that had attempted to kill Gareth. Her energy was still. Had I actually separated them?

Remi reluctantly set me down, but he stuck close to my side as I hurried over to Gareth, checking him over. His wounds had healed, just shiny new pink scars in their place.

"Hadi did this?" I asked, running my fingers over the largest new scar on his chest. Using a silver blade as she had, he could've bled out before this had healed.

"I won't go into detail of how he did it," said Gareth, his mouth twisting in a grimace.

My eyes went to Hadi and I offered him a smile, which he returned. It was subtle, which I was coming to realize was the norm for him, but when he did show expression, I found it spoke volumes more.

"Spit and fire," Andrus said, chuckling.

"What?" I asked.

Andrus jerked his head at Gareth. "Dragons typically use a combination of spit and fire to heal."

"There's herbs and things involved, too," Gareth added hastily. He looked at me, a bit green around the gills. "He doesn't just spit into an open wound."

Nausea almost choked his words off and I grinned, that grin becoming a sly smile. "Does spit gross you out?"

His eyes widened, horrified for different reasons than usual. "Of course it does. It doesn't disgust you?" He made a gagging noise and took a deep breath, shaking his head. "Let's stop talking about it, please."

I delighted in this new piece of information I'd learned about my mate. Big strong wolf that's seen any number or horrific things, and it's spit that gets his gorge?

It just made me love him that little bit more.

Arthur was sitting in the same place he had been, not making a move toward Sasha's prone form lying sprawled at Hadi's feet. The look on his face was pure agony and my heart twisted. He was torn, truly devastated by the circumstances.

As hard as this was for me, I couldn't imagine what he was going through. In his mind, it was only a few days ago that he'd seen his wife. It was just another normal day, until I pulled him into a reality in a future he hadn't even had time to contemplate. And then she's here, his past reestablished itself before he could even think about the future.

And then she left him.

"She's moving," said Hadi.

All of us whipped around and stared as Sasha began to stir. Her eyes stayed closed as her limbs twitched and bent, her fingers gripping into the muck as they spasmed like some demented spider. She flipped over violently onto her side, eyes still shut tight, face impassive, as her hair whipped forward and splayed onto the ground like a pot of ink had been splashed over her head.

A groan issued low in her throat, turning into a croaking... laugh?

Hadi took a step back, hands raised and ready to attack when her body flipped over onto her back and her eyes sprang open. All of us were on our feet as she cackled and stood in a slow, demented motion, her puppet strings taken back up by some invisible hand.

"What the fuck?" I whispered.

Sasha's head snapped in my direction, and I flinched, backing up several paces. The hatred in her eyes was pure and unrelenting. The icy blue changed to green, changed to orange, the light in them dancing in the gloom, rimmed by bloodshot speckles.

A cold breeze ripped across the bank from the river, swirling around us, voices whispering from the darkness of the trees that crept closer around with every blink.

I drew up my defenses, as did my mates. I was soon standing with a half-wolf, a vampire, a gargoyle, and a half-dragon.

When she spoke, it was with a wheezing voice, every breath a struggle. She had to fight to get the words out, two hissing, creaking, barely formed syllables for every strangled breath.

"You think you're clever," she said, her head at a wholly unnatural angle. "You think you're clever."

She continued to say it, her whole body jerking and twitching as the demon figured out the operating instructions.

Then she stopped.

The stillness was worse.

Her head was bowed, that curtain of hair falling in a wave almost to the ground. Sasha drew herself up, rolling her shoulders as she settled into her skin. A new intelligence was looking back at us out of her eyes.

"Twixt?" I asked

The demon's eyes widened, and an animalistic growl crackled in the back of his throat. His head tilted slowly to the side. "Clever."

Movement in the trees drew my eye, and I breathed a sigh of relief when Death appeared, Felix in tow. Twixt shot them a glare, before turning his attention back to me.

"Have you been inside Sasha's body this whole time?" I asked. I needed to know. Arthur needed to know.

Sasha smiled, her grin spreading far too wide. "Yes," the demon hissed.

Arthur made a strangled noise but still made no move. There was a small modicum of relief that washed over me, happy at least to have an answer. But I had brought this thing with us. I'd let it into Death's house.

The smile on its face fell, turning back to that malicious sneer. "You should have let me kill him." Twixt jutted his chin toward Gareth. "It would've been easier."

Death stepped forward. "Why?"

The demon didn't answer, and the concussion of the spell Death threw at him washed over us. The demon sputtered, trying to fight the binding, but failed. He had no choice but to talk now.

Twixt rolled Sasha's neck on her shoulders, head lolling to the side as he appraised the egregore. "Because now the rest of your deaths will all be more painful."

CHAPTER TWELVE

Bel

"No," I whispered. "Why would they punish you. You didn't do anything."

Norah stroked my face, and I trembled at her touch. "But they know it will hurt you. Being in your orbit is a sentence of pain for everyone."

"What can I do?" I pleaded, voice cracking. "How do I get you out?"

My mother crouched in front of me and pulled me to her, resting my head against her chest like she had so many times when I was a child. To comfort me or shield me from my father's wrath.

"That's not our destiny. We're here with you. Forever." She hushed me as I choked back a sob. "The others will be joining us soon."

"Others?" I asked, looking around frantically for more shapes lurching out of the deeper darkness.

"Your sister," my mother cooed. "Your friends. Your generals. Your confidants. Your father."

I stiffened. If anyone deserved to be here, it was him. Not these women. Not any of the others either.

"Why?" I asked, pulling away. "I haven't done anything more terrible than my father has done. Was he taunted with the torture of his loved ones? If he ever had any."

"It's not important," said Norah. "This is all about you. You finally got your wish."

"Wish." A cold, creeping doubt was worming its way up from the back of my mind. "My goals were never about me. They were always about the greater good."

"Just because you tell yourself that, doesn't make it true," Norah said pityingly. "It's always been about you. Everyone you take into your life is subject to your will. You wouldn't have it any other way."

"No—"

"We could have had a long, happy life together," she continued. "Our child would've been born. Your kingdom would've survived. Wouldn't it have been worth bowing to the Titans to have those things?" Her long sigh coiled around me. "Just think about what could've been."

"I did what I had to do."

"You did what you *wanted* to do," Norah corrected. "You knew in your heart that it would only end badly, but you figured as long as you were still standing you could throw as many other Ætherim into the meat grinder as you pleased. You hadn't planned on how close they would be to the city."

Her boney hand grabbed my face. "We were in danger, in the direct line of fire, and you didn't stop. You didn't think about how *we* would suffer! It's all your fault!"

"No!" I shouted, scrambling away. I got to my feet and stayed there this time, the pounding in my head manageable compared to the fear that gripped me. I ran.

The women shrieked, but I didn't hear them pursue. I made it to the line of shelter I'd been aiming for originally and found it to be a rocky grotto with an ice-cold pool in the middle, stinking of rot. I tripped and my foot slipped in, coming back covered in slime.

I skirted around the edge, trying to find an opening on the other side. I was alive, this body was as real and whole as it had ever been. If this was one of the seven hells, there had to be an exit. I just had to find it. The living couldn't be kept here.

A hand broke from the water and grabbed my ankle, pulling me down. My chin cracked on the ground before I was yanked into the water. A mouthful of the fetid soup made it down my throat before I clamped it shut tight. I needed air, I needed to get to the surface, I—

I didn't need to breathe. I stopped struggling, floating in the brine and realized my body wasn't screaming for air. But just as I calmed, a new fear stabbed into my chest as the creature that had grabbed my ankle floated up from the depths to hover in front of me. A hand shot out and wrapped long fingers around my throat.

My father's face loomed into view, just as ghastly as the others, but this time it elicited only a blind rage.

"Hello, whelp."

I struck out, grabbing him around the throat. I lost a lot of force being underwater, but I wrenched his head to the side, cracking his neck and leaving his head at an odd angle. I kicked for the surface while he laughed, swimming languidly after me, not rushed in the least.

When my head popped out of the water, I took in a reflexive gasp of air even though I hadn't needed it. I clawed at the bank, pulling myself up and out, water sloshing onto the rocky ground. My father's hand reappeared, snatching at my leg, but I dodged, pressing myself against the wall.

He was laughing as he rose from the water and I ran, tripping and stumbling the whole way. His wet footsteps followed, still slow and measured. He wasn't worried about my escape.

I would never escape him.

Chapter Thirteen

Arthur

My wife was gone. There was nothing left that I recognized as I looked at this horrible monster that had tried to murder Gareth, and would have done gods' know what else if she hadn't been caught.

Sasha had a brilliant smile that made my heart happy every time she blessed me with it. Now it was broken and chipped and blackened with blood. The bright eyes that sparkled with mischief were an acidic shade of orange, burning with hate.

Her voice greeted me in the morning, and it was the last sweet thing I heard before I went to sleep. The sounds this creature made were the stuff of nightmares.

I couldn't stop crying.

Sasha kept me sane. I loved her more than anyone. I'd given up hope of ever fulfilling my purpose, but she gave me a new one. She may have been human, but I looked forward to our lives together. And when she was old and gray, I would care for her just the same.

I barely heard the words as she went back and forth with Meg, the harsh timbre blending into a drone that ate at my sanity. This couldn't be real.

The demon turned its eyes on me, and I flinched.

"Aww," it simpered. "Sasha didn't want any part of this, you know. She proclaimed her love for you until I silenced her."

I shook uncontrollably. Meg stepped in front of me, facing the demon. "Stop it," she snapped at it. "Leave him out of this. Tell us what the hell you want."

The demon sneered. "I already told you. I wanted to kill the wolf."

"Why?" Andrus asked, subtly trying to support Gareth as he shook and sweated from the effort of standing.

"All of chaos needs you dead, and I want to speed things up a bit," said the demon, rolling his eyes. "Catch up."

"They're trying to stop us?" Andrus asked.

The demon only blinked at him.

"Why would they do that?" asked Meg. "Your kind was behind my creation, right?"

The demon shrugged.

"So why try to stop me now?" she asked.

"You were a means to an end. We never wanted the Titans freed."

"I'm afraid I don't follow," she said.

"When you paid the Titans a visit and foiled their original plans, the countdown began. We needed to get you to that point. Now that it's done, you are no longer necessary."

"There was a contingency?" Death asked, voice barely above a whisper.

Twixt nodded. "A Hexengate."

Death paled, but the rest of us could only wait for more of an explanation. After shaking off his initial shock, he looked around, mouth agape.

"An ancient magick. They are sentient portals, given a purpose and set loose to fulfill it however they see fit. Nothing good has ever come from one."

"Just absolute chaos," said the demon, smiling wider.

"Keep talking," snapped Death.

Twixt sighed. "Once the Titans decided their plan was no longer viable, they hit the kill switch. I'm not sure how long it'll take, but I'm getting impatient, and I saw an opportunity." It looked at Death. "You should really upgrade the wards on your own house. It was far too easy to grab the elf."

He laughed and Death hit him with a warning, choking him off. "Fine," it snarled, rubbing its neck. "The entire idea was that all the powers their construct possessed would be released from the vessel and fed into the gate. It's been sitting there this whole time, waiting its turn. It will activate after it feeds and after that... it's anyone's guess. The Titans will be mighty surprised when it doesn't free them like they planned."

The demon looked at Meg and licked its lips. "Since the construct is ours, that gate is too." It tapped its chin. "My money is on good ol' fashioned carnage and the breakdown of society, even though that's already well underway. They seem confident that war is about to break out with humans, and I've heard that the human military is packing some innovative new weaponry." It rubbed its hands together in anticipation.

"But why go after Gareth like that would solve the issue?" Remi asked.

"Because he was the first," said the demon. "The first mate. Get rid of him, the other bonds fall apart." He blinked. "They aren't strong enough to withstand the loss."

"Then Meg becomes vulnerable enough that the gate can draw her in?" Andrus guessed.

"Yes," said the demon. "Now the process will be drawn out and painful. Not that I care about that bit. That's a problem for you, not me. The problem is, I hate to wait."

"I think we have everything we need, don't you?" Death asked.

He didn't wait for an answer. He disappeared and reappeared right in front of Twixt, slapping a hand to the creature's forehead.

I closed my eyes and looked away as Sasha fell to the ground, shifting and changing, not able to hold a form.

"Show yourself, Twixt," said Death. It was a command given with no sense of urgency, but Sasha screamed, jaw dislocating. The sound cut off as a misty figure forced its way out, coalescing into a human shape.

"What are you going to do?" it asked. "I haven't broken any treatises."

"You trespassed in my home. My turf, my rules," said Death.

"Wait—" said Twixt, throwing out his hands. Lifting just one finger, Death pointed at the demon, and it was pulled apart in every direction.

As soon as he was gone, I dropped to my knees at Sasha's side, grabbing her hand and holding it tight to my chest, wiping the blood and gore from her face. There was nothing recognizable about her except her eyes as they fluttered open. I pushed matted hair from her forehead and caressed her cheek. "Sasha?" I asked, my voice cracking.

Bleeding lips bent into a pained smile as her gaze focused on me. Her words were so soft that I had to bend close to her mouth to hear. "Arthur," she breathed. Her voice hitched as her eyes welled with tears. "I'm sorry."

I dropped her hand and grabbed her frail body in my arms, cradling her tightly. "You have nothing to be sorry for."

"I tried to fight—" A cough racked her body and I thought she'd shake apart.

"Shhh," I said, running my hand up and down her back at a slow, methodical pace. "None of this is your fault."

She struggled to take in a breath. Her body was too broken, too weak. Even Hadi wouldn't be able to heal her now.

My chest ached. My Sasha would die here and there was nothing I could do. I failed to keep her safe. But at least she wouldn't be alone.

"Do you remember the field of wildflowers?" I asked her, tears rolling freely down my face.

She looked ahead at some distant point that I couldn't see. "Where you first told me you loved me." The lightness of her touch as she reached for my face broke me. A sob broke loose and I had to fight to regain control.

"I wish for you to be surrounded by wildflowers," I said with a quivering smile. "And love and happiness. You will be reunited with your family, and you will know only joy for eternity. You brought me so much of it in this life." I kissed her forehead. "You deserve nothing but bliss in the next."

Her brow knit together and she gave me the all-knowing glance that always cut right to my soul. "I know what waits for me will be wonderful," she said. With a gentle smile she wiped the tears from my face. "But you also deserve joy."

Sasha motioned to Meg, who hesitantly moved to join us and crouched down beside me. "You can finally fulfill your purpose." Her smile grew wider. "And I'm so glad that I could see you reunited with your family."

Meg choked with a sob of her own as she took Sasha's proffered hand.

"I'm glad it's you," she said to Meg. "I know you'll love him as much as I do."

Meg could only nod, tears running into the corners of her smile.

Sasha turned back to me. "May you find peace, Arthur. Please be happy. I will be."

"I love you," I said.

"And always," she replied.

Her eyes drifted closed and her face fell into a peaceful repose. I sensed another pair of eyes on me and looked up to see Sasha's soul, freed from her body. There was the woman I knew, light radiating around her. Death stepped forward then and without a word she went to join him.

"I'll deliver her personally," he assured me.

With one last smile over her shoulder, Death ushered her through a portal, and she was gone.

I broke down, clinging to Sasha and rocking back and forth as I sobbed. Meg placed a supportive hand on my shoulder and squeezed before moving back to the others, where they drifted away to give me space to grieve.

CHAPTER FOURTEEN

Meg

I lost track of how much time had passed as we stood aside, huddled together as Arthur grieved over Sasha. At some point Death returned and encouraged us to go back to the house. He would deal with Arthur.

Feeling helpless in this situation—I was better at consoling people when I wasn't also grieving—we complied, beginning the long trek home. We didn't speed along. I couldn't bring myself to rush, and the others didn't seem inclined either. Felix did tarry along behind, casting glances back every now and again.

"You should go back, if that's what you feel is right," I said. "You know him the best."

Felix shook his head. "This is all beyond me. I wouldn't be of any use to him right now."

Gareth's hand moved to one of the stab marks on his chest, already getting lost among the others. He looked at Andrus and Felix. "Did you have any weird thoughts while you were stuck in... whatever it was Twixt did?"

Andrus shook his head. "There was an uncanny feeling, but I was just walking on an endless road." His eyes widened and he stopped. "Shit. I never got the stuff Death needed for the bonding."

A small stab of pain hit me. "I'm not sure that's going to happen soon, anyway. It'll be alright."

Felix looked uncomfortable. "I got to thinking. That's always dangerous. I was trying to figure out which one of you was playing a prank on me. It took me a minute to figure out that's not what it was." He scratched the back of his head. "I probably should've done this a long time ago, but I'm sorry. For all the 'pranks' I pulled." He made air quotes with his fingers. "I was an asshole."

"You're still an asshole," said Remi with a grunt. "But I appreciate the apology."

The others nodded and Andrus nudged Felix with his elbow. "Some introspection did you good, huh?"

Felix punched at him, laughing. "You were my first guess as to who did it. All that spiritual bullshit."

"But I was right, regardless," said Andrus, ducking another punch and dancing back a few paces.

Gareth was watching with a frown.

"I take it your experience wasn't so enlightening?" I asked.

"My wolf took over. All of that possessiveness." He shook his head. "I probably would've killed any of my brothers if you had gotten in my way in that mindset." He looked at me out of the corner of his eye and I took his hand.

"I know that's not you," I said.

His shoulders relaxed, and his entire posture eased as we walked, but he only nodded, giving my hand a squeeze back.

"We know who you really are," said Andrus, a smile in his voice. "All bark and no bite."

Gareth chuckled. "Next full moon, catch me outside."

The intense gloom that had been hanging over us lightened.

"I'm almost happy for him," said Remi.

"Arthur?" Felix asked, brow knitting into a deep furrow.

The gargoyle nodded. "At least this way he gets to say goodbye. He gets closure. And he found out the truth, so that won't be haunting him forever. It may seem like a callous thing to say, but—" He shrugged.

"Closure is a powerful thing," said Hadi. He had been stone silent the entire walk, but not in his usual way. It was more pensive, lost in his thoughts. "This will help him heal."

We all lapsed back into silence after that.

Once we return to the house, we all settled back in the kitchen, picking at leftovers and wondering where we went from here. There was no way we could just set off on a journey through the realms of Hell so quickly after this, but what was the appropriate time to grieve when the clock was literally ticking?

"What do you make of this Hexengate situation?" I asked. They hadn't been much time to give it thought before, but the way Twixt spoke of it, I was in extreme peril, and there was no telling when my time would run out.

"Can you reach out to the Titans? Tell them to hold off?" Remi asked.

"I can certainly try. But the way it sounded to me was that it was already underway. You didn't see the looks on the Titan's faces. Kronos was positive that I'd failed. That the entire thing was blown because of my mistake."

"Not your mistake," said Felix. "The chaos demons were interfering, same as they have been this entire time."

Andrus nodded. "Nichelle was a perfect candidate for possession. She was so far gone, it wouldn't have taken much, and we didn't suspect a thing."

"Reaching out to the Titans now would be a mistake."

We all turned to find Death standing in the doorway. Arthur was nowhere to be seen.

He gave a tired smile. "I sent him to get some rest." He walked in and took a seat at the table, groaning as he settled in. "You know, when I first approached you all about joining Team Death, I didn't think it would bring this much trouble to my doorstep. Literally, in this case."

His words weren't accusatory, just tired. "What Twixt said was correct. The contingency plan has been enacted."

"How do you know?" Gareth asked.

"Once I knew what I was looking for, it wasn't hard to find. There is a Hexengate all set up and waiting to be fed."

"Shit," I cursed. "How much time?"

Before my body is dissolved into nothing and the cosmic dust that's left is absorbed by a sentient portal that could release a new hell on earth. But I didn't say that out loud.

Death shrugged. "There's no way of knowing. I doubt even the Titans know. You can conjure the gates, but once you activate them, they run on their own schedule."

"So there's no way of stopping it?" Remi asked.

Death heaved a sigh. "The only thing that will stop it, is accomplishing what that gate was programmed to do. Free the Titans from Tartarus. It's the ultimate failsafe."

"But if the demons are controlling it," I said.

Death shook his head. "That only works if you're absorbed by the gate. Then they could control it."

"Oh," I said. That makes it better.

"Then we get this job finished," Gareth said. "We do what we've been trying to all along."

"Yes. That is your only option." Death shook his head. "But even then, there's no guarantee it will stop the gate. It just won't eat *you*." At our horrified expressions, he elaborated. "It's sentient. If it is of a mind to open, it will. Its end goal might change, so there's no telling what might happen when it does. We are all at its whim right now." His words dripped with bitterness. "It's a hell of a thing to do to ensure your freedom. I can't blame them, but at the same time, they're putting all of us at risk. Something they claimed to never want to do."

I looked around at my mates. Their faces held the entire gamut of emotion, from grief to anger, and no small amount of betrayal.

"It goes against everything they swore to us," said Andrus. "We gave them our fealty because we believed in their cause. But rather than try again, or reevaluate, they would risk the lives that they were supposedly bound to protect? This is no better than what the Ætherim would've done."

Death nodded. "Do remember that to their minds you are very insubstantial." He held up his hand to stave off protest. "I don't mean it as an insult. I mean, never in a million years would it cross their minds to consult with creatures so much lower on the food chain. You failed in your directive, so that was the end of the story. They gave up, and turned to their backup plan. To them, you aren't capable of pulling a rabbit out of a hat. Your worth has been called into question."

"Then I guess we just have to prove them wrong," I said. There was nothing else for it. It was either try and win, try and fail, or do nothing and die.

"Unfortunately, this will rush things that shouldn't be rushed," said Death. "Arthur needs more time to recover if his head is going to be where it needs to be. And we need to plan."

I took a deep breath, refusing to let the gravity of the situation rattle my nerves. We could only do what we could do, and if the Hexengate activated before we made it to Tartarus, well… it was a good run.

"You should all get some rest," said Death. More than one of us had a dubious look on our face. "I'm serious. You need to have clear heads, and you're not accomplishing that half-dead on your feet."

I nodded reluctantly, the exhaustion pulling at me even as I tried to deny how tired I was. "First thing tomorrow then."

My mates all nodded their agreement, and we went off toward our rooms.

CHAPTER FIFTEEN

Hadi

I couldn't fall asleep. My eyes felt raw and red as I tossed around, staring at the ceiling, getting up, pacing the floor, going back to bed, forcing my eyes shut and hoping sleep would come. But it wouldn't.

All I could think about was Meg. Our conversation earlier had felt so natural, and we'd fallen into step so seamlessly. She'd taken control the moment she realized her mates were in danger. She'd balked at being carried by my claws, but it was a healthy respect for the precarious position she would be in, at the whims of a massively powerful creature. Fear hadn't played a part in it, until we reached about three thousand feet.

There were several other positions I'd also enjoy putting her in.

I growled in frustration and turned to my other side, trying to block out thoughts of her on her knees, looking up at me before—

"Dammit," I grumbled, throwing back the covers and stalking out of the room. There was a pool outside, maybe a quick dip in cold water would shock some sense back into me.

I'd been a high priest for so long, and part of that was celibacy. It made the task of avoiding getting attached to anyone easier, but despite the conclusions that most people came to upon meeting me—that I was a cold, intimidating alpha that had no use for emotions—in reality, I hungered for connection. I avoided it because it was a liability I couldn't afford.

But Meg was no damsel that would be left vulnerable every time I went off to fight. She would be right there beside me in the battle. She'd already proved that.

I turned the corner and heard voices up ahead. Meg and Remi. I continued on my way, determined to walk by and not interrupt. Mostly because I didn't trust my cock to behave itself. Now wasn't the time.

"Hadi," Meg called as I passed by.

I stepped back and hovered in the doorway, making it clear I intended to be on my way. Meg was sitting with her legs slung over Remi's lap as she rested against one of the large pillows that dotted the room. One of his hands rested on her thigh while the other massaged her feet.

This seemed to be some kind of lounging area, filled with overstuffed furniture that looked out of place compared to the rest of the house. Low lights burned in the back two corners of the room, leaving just enough illumination for ambience.

"Couldn't sleep either?" I asked them.

They shook their heads. "I'm exhausted, but my mind won't slow down," said Meg.

"I was planning on taking a walk, and found Meg on the way," said Remi. "We were having a terribly boring conversation, but it didn't do its job."

Meg smiled. "Because we're not capable of being boring." She looked at me. "You're welcome to join."

I hesitated, my gaze lingering on her legs, her hips, the swell of her breasts through the thin shirt she wore. I was about to refuse when I caught her scent.

Remi had also stilled, watching Meg intently. When I looked back to Meg, her eyes met and held mine and my breath caught in my throat. She had the same need, the hunger that I felt.

"Is it wrong?" she asked, concern overshadowing the desire. "I don't want to disrespect the dead, but... I need the intimacy. All I want is to be with my mates."

I had to swallow a few times before I could form the words. "Not at all," I assured her.

She held her hand out to me and I crossed the room in a flash. She stood to greet me and pressed me down onto the cushion she'd just vacated, straddling my hips. One hand rested on her waist and I cupped the back of her head with my other, pulling her to me for a kiss.

She sighed against my lips, a chaste beginning transforming into a consuming fire. I parted her lips with my tongue and tangled it with hers as she ground against me, teasing my cock to full attention. She dropped her head down and flicked her tongue across my nipple. I groaned. Meg kissed her way back up my chest, nipping at my neck with her... fangs.

I gasped and she stopped, running her tongue over her teeth. I ran the pad of my thumb across her lower lip. "They told me about this, but..." With just the slightest press against her fang, I felt my skin break. I tore it open a little more and Meg's tongue darted out to taste it.

Her hips bucked into me as her eyes rolled back, her moan of ecstasy almost making me come by itself. Meg ripped at my pants and pulled my cock free before slipping out of her panties and throwing them aside. She took one look at my size and grinned wickedly, leaning in to speak against my ear.

"I like a challenge," she said, before lining me up and sinking slowly down without pause, breathing deeply when she bottomed out. She took a moment to adjust and began to move, riding me with increasing speed. Her fangs scraped my neck, and I held her head there, wordlessly begging for her bite.

She obliged, sinking her teeth into my throat. The pleasure was blinding but I wouldn't let myself come. Not yet. There was motion at the door and Gareth entered the room, followed by Andrus and Felix.

"This is exactly my preferred way to tire myself out," said Felix, desire radiating off him.

Meg drank deeply, rising almost all the way to my tip before sinking back down. She licked the bite until it closed and rose off me. I reached for her in protest, but she was merely changing things up.

Remi had been watching and slowly administering to himself, but when Meg motioned for him to join, he sprang into action. Meg got down on her knees and spread my legs wide, licking my shaft while Remi placed himself behind her.

I watched with hooded eyes as a bead of sweat ran down her chest, as her face contorted with pleasure as Remi entered her from behind. She gripped my knees, letting Remi build up his pace, her perfect breasts bouncing with every thrust he made. Magick swept through the room. The bonding.

Once he found a consistent rhythm, a sensation swept across my skin, a prickling fire hot and cold at the same time, and Meg's eyes became a swirling rainbow of color. I felt her magick rise and sweep through the room.

She dipped her head and licked my tip before swallowing my cock. My hands curled in her hair as I encouraged her to take more, a challenge she readily accepted. With small pumps of my hips she took all of me, bracing against my thighs as my thrusts became more significant.

Remi's hand snaked around to finger her clit and she came, moaning around my cock. That was more than I could take, and I followed suit in time with Remi.

She pulled back from me, but I felt no different. Gareth noticed the look of disappointment on my face and shook his head. "We all need to be involved before the bond can take effect for you." He chuckled. "Get ready for round two."

"Maybe three," said Meg with a wink, turning to Andrus.

"How would you like it?" he asked.

"Surprise me," she said.

Andrus looked around and pulled a side table away from the wall, sweeping her up in his arms and sitting her on the edge. Her legs wrapped tight around him and he buried his fangs in her neck as he drove into her. She leaned back and Felix was there, bending to catch her nipple in his mouth while he pinched the other one between his fingers, eliciting a moan. She reached for his cock and stroked him. I watched as they all moved together seamlessly, knowing what each of them would do and adjusting for it.

Her cries became silent screams as Andrus spurred his pace, her pleasure peaking and all she could do was ride it out. When Andrus finished, Meg released her grip on Felix and he hurriedly repositioned her, bending her over the long edge of the table. He eased into her, gave a few fast strokes and pulled out before hitching her hips and spreading her cheeks.

Meg's head bowed as Felix pushed deeper into her ass with every exhale. There was a pulse that must've been a communication between them because Gareth moved forward and stood in front of her. She braced herself more firmly on her elbows and licked his shaft, grabbing his hips as he stepped into her, pushing past her lips and down her throat in one smooth movement.

Gareth and Felix timed their thrusts so they rammed home in unison. Meg's body was covered in a thin sheen of sweat and she pulled away from Gareth as her whole body tensed. She gripped the edge of the table as it rocked against the floor, mouth falling open with a gasp. She reached back and stroked the tip of Felix's ear and he growled, hiking his hips. One of his hands moved between her legs, circling her clit.

Her moans were music, and I was rock hard again as Felix buried his face in her shoulder, crying out as they came together. Once her legs stopped shaking, Felix moved back, and Gareth scooped her up. She grinned at him, breathing hard as he knelt on some pillows and positioned himself behind her, pulling her against his chest. Her knees rested on either side of his.

"Hadi," she said. I blinked out of my reverie as Gareth ran his nose along the sensitive skin behind her ear, nipping her earlobe as he lifted her enough to slide slowly into her ass.

She gasped, breathing deep before bobbing on Gareth's cock.

"You can join if you'd like," she said, riding him faster, building her pleasure. I considered. Two alphas sharing a mate at the same time? Her eyes slipped closed and she bit her lip as they found a good pace. Gareth only had eyes for her, but when I did manage to catch his gaze he didn't give me a territorial warning glare.

The bonding magick ran over my skin, calling to me.

I joined them.

I kneeled in front of Meg, capturing a nipple in my mouth as she slowed to allow for another repositioning. Her pussy clenched around me as I entered her and we all found a new rhythm, alternating our strokes.

Meg rolled her nipples between her fingers as we moved together, the stimulation bringing her close to another climax. Gareth's thrusts were shorter and harder as he reached his peak and he came, Meg bucking harder against me as she found her release.

Gareth moved back and she continued riding me.

Her gaze roved over me as her hands found the ridges of scales that ran along my hips and chest, transforming her hands into claws and running them up and down as she traced each scale.

I groaned, reaching down and circling her clit as she spread her knees wider, taking all of me to the hilt.

The magick snapped around us, licking over my skin as she slowly took more of me in. Finally, she bottomed out, breathing hard. I tilted her face up to kiss her and she smiled.

"Doing alright?" I asked, genuinely concerned. The last thing I wanted to do was hurt her.

She took my face in her hands, beginning to move. "Yes."

I met her stroke for stroke with small thrusts, taking great care for any sign that it was too much.

But I needn't have worried. She kept picking up speed, adjusting to my size. She threw her head back and moaned, grabbing my shoulders for better purchase as she lifted herself higher before driving back down. I pumped into her harder.

"Gods, yes," she moaned.

We crashed together and she screamed my name, her entire body shaking from head to toe with her release.

Three more hard thrusts and I followed, filling her. The bond solidified and I could suddenly feel her emotions as well as echoes of the other's and for a moment I was overwhelmed. Her head lolled side to side as she came down, the haze in her eyes clear confirmation that I'd done my job well.

When we separated at last, breathing heavily and still running our hands all over each other, I realized someone else had joined our gathering.

Arthur was standing there, leaning against the doorframe, face impassive—but I could see the longing in his eyes, not for sex but for closeness, connection.

Meg shook as I took one more taste of her, licked the sweat from her neck. We were all watching him warily. Through the bond—I realized with amazement that it was already strengthening—I could feel how much she wanted him, but how afraid she was to ask.

Arthur walked into the room and Meg, with a final caress of my face, stood. They met in the middle, and Arthur took her hand, guiding it to his chest and over his heart.

The magick was still raging through the room and it coalesced around Meg, unsure as she was of how to proceed. Arthur placed a light kiss on her forehead, before resting his head against hers and placing his hand over her heart.

"I promise all of me to you, as soon as I'm able to give it," he whispered.

The bonding magick swelled, and they both gasped as it flooded into him, taking him in, making him a part of us wholly. All of us were shocked into stillness as the power within us ratcheted up to an unbelievable height.

The ties that linked us all together had seemed like silk strands, unbreakable but ethereal. Now those ties had been infused with iron. We were finally complete. A single unit.

A family.

"Wow," said Meg, huffing out a laugh.

Arthur chuckled and wrapped her in his arms. "And it's only the beginning," he said.

The rest of us were left staring at each other, sharing looks of amazement or just grinning stupidly as we were taken by the implications of this night.

"Kind of anticlimactic," Felix mumbled. "Now it's just a room full of sweaty, naked dudes while the charmer over there wins the day."

CHAPTER SIXTEEN

Meg

I woke up to Death clearing his throat. I was sandwiched between Hadi and Gareth, the others arrayed around us on the giant stack of pillows we'd thrown on the floor. We'd cobbled together a bunch of blankets and were sharing them amongst ourselves.

"Must you sully my pillows? I can't clean those."

I shrugged, a satisfied smirk on my face. "None of the beds were big enough for all of us and we didn't want to separate yet."

I looked around at my mates, starting to stir. Arthur was on the outer edge, Felix's hand having flopped onto his face sometime in the night. As I watched, his eyes opened, narrowing as he realized. He lifted the hand off his face and returned it to Felix's side with a, "Do you mind?"

"Not at all," Felix grumbled, still half asleep. His head popped up. "Wait, what?"

"I thought I told you to get some rest," said Death.

"We had to be tired first," Andrus said, shrugging his shoulders matter-of-factly. "I slept like a baby. Haven't felt this rested in a long time."

"That still doesn't excuse what you've done to my lounge," said Death, crossing his arms over his chest.

"Send us the bill," said Gareth, giving me a kiss before he got to his feet, sans blankets.

Death rolled his eyes and turned away down the hall, calling over his shoulder, "When you're ready to do some actual work, join me in the dining room."

Felix huffed. "What's he talking about. What we did last night was *hard* work."

Hadi's arm tightened around my waist as I laughed. "I'd like to do some more, right now," he said. "But alas..."

"We both need showers, right?" I said, running my hand over his chest. "You're welcome to join me."

Andrus propped up on his elbows. "You guys ever notice how much she likes water?"

"I'm already planning for it," said Felix. He ticked everything off on his fingers. "Our house needs a pool, a sauna, a hot tub, a huge shower, a soaking tub, maybe another pool..."

Gareth looked at Andrus. "A private hot spring nearby."

"Definitely," agreed Andrus.

Hadi purred and scooped me up, carrying me off toward the bathroom. It was nice and spacious, elegantly simple. Green tile and glass all the way around.

"You'll have to show me how to use this," he said, looking uncertainly at the modern hardware.

I obliged, getting the shower warming up while Hadi held me close, running his hands across my hips, up my sides and over my breasts, the light skimming sensation more arousing than I could have imagined.

As soon as the water was hot, I pulled him in after me. Death had a good supply of high-end soaps and shampoos, so we were spoiled for choice. I chose a luxurious sandalwood and tobacco scent for Hadi, and he picked a jasmine scent for me.

"Just like the garden," he said.

He soaped me up first, taking care over my breasts, lavishing each with attention as he rinsed me off before moving on to my hips.

Hadi ran the loofa down my stomach, across my hips, around my thighs, teasing before finally sliding it between my legs, lathering and fingering at the same time. He dropped the sponge, turning me around and moving two fingers into my channel as he pressed me tight against him, his cock straining against my lower back.

He pumped his long fingers into me, getting me nice and wet before pulling out. I pouted but he grabbed the shower-head, aiming one of the lighter jets at my clit before three fingers dipped back inside me.

I panted, my peak approaching fast until I came, slapping my hands against the wall as my knees buckled. Hadi nipped my throat and pushed my weight forward onto my hands as he retrieved the loofa, cleaning my back and spending extra time on my thighs and ass.

I gasped as his fingers trailed lightly across my shoulder blades, gooseflesh rising from the sensation, but Hadi's surprised grunt made me pause.

"What is it?" I asked, turning around.

"Wait," he said, running his fingers over my skin again. This time the sensation of goosebumps was stronger, and it lingered.

I frowned. "Is something happening?"

He laughed and the joy in it made me turn to face him.

"You have scales!" He studied my torso and skimmed his fingers across me. Before my eyes, I watched scales in the familiar scallop pattern appear on my skin.

My jaw dropped.

Violet scales, flashing indigo when the light caught them right. They covered my abdomen, trailing down my hips, and traveling straight up over my heart.

"They're in a curved pattern on your shoulders as well, all the way down to your hips. Protecting the vital areas," he said. The joy on his face was contagious. "You are even more beautiful," he said, kissing me fiercely and backing me against the wall.

"How did I get so lucky?" He knelt in front of me and hooked my right knee over his shoulder, glancing up at me before swiping his tongue through my center and swirling it around my clit. My hands went to fist in his hair, but he didn't have any, so I settled for gently pressing him to me, running my hands along his smooth scalp.

Suddenly his tongue forked and dove deep into my core. I cried out, the sensation consuming as both sides moved independently, seeking out places that had never been touched.

His tongue plunged into me with a frenzy, the growls and purrs coming from him so fucking hot that his deep thrust and deeper moan had me coming again, harder than last time.

He stood and I grabbed his cock, stroking slowly. I was just getting on my knees when another strange sensation came over me and I toppled back as a bunch of weight pulled at me.

Hadi's mouth dropped open and he was shocked silent. I looked at my reflection in the foggy glass door and clapped a hand to my mouth.

I had a tail, curling gracefully on the floor. But the real shock was the pair of wings folded against my back. My head snapped to Hadi and he threw back his head with a throaty laugh.

"Wh—" I said, before stopping short as a small rivulet of flame burst from my mouth.

"Oh, Megiste," he said, grabbing my hips and yanking me to him. "The things I can teach you."

His passion reached a boiling point, and he pinned me against the wall, mindful of my wings, my thighs rising to rest on his hips as I wrapped my legs tight around him.

His cock throbbed as he thrust into me, my pussy clenching around him as he found his rhythm, driving hard and fast as my pleasure escalated along with my volume.

Hadi plunged so deep I saw stars. Luckily my fire breathing calmed down so I didn't burn down the bathroom as I screamed. My thighs shook as he ravished me with pure and simple ferocity. My tail lashed around his leg much like his had the day we met, and I was surprised how easy it was to learn to control it. There were ridges but no spikes on the end and I grinned wickedly as I moved my tail to caress the underside of his balls.

My dragon shuddered and groaned, crushing his lips to mine as his pace reached fever pitch and I screamed my release, Hadi following close behind.

By the time the last aftershocks were gone, I'd shifted back to my regular form.

"As enjoyable as that was, I'm not going to need sex to bring out the shift, am I?" I asked with a grin, once we'd untangled from each other and finished the actual bathing we were here to do. "That could be inconvenient."

"I don't think so." He grinned. "But we'll just have to practice everything to find out."

CHAPTER SEVENTEEN

Meg

About an hour later we were all clean and dressed and ready to talk strategy, even if we were still a bit punchy from the bonding. The tone turned somber quickly once the gravity of what was at stake settled in.

"These are the facts that we know," said Death. "The clock is ticking, a Hexengate is preparing to open, you haven't seen the last of the chaos demons, you will have to make it through the bottom four layers of hell before you get to Tartarus, and then you'll have to find a way past the gate when the original plan to open it has already been sabotaged." He paused. "And let's not forget that Belsioch is still out there somewhere, and I'm sure once he finds his way back, he'll be madder than ever."

"I'm waiting for the peptalk," Arthur said.

Death sighed. "You're not getting one. There is very little room for error, and you'll be lucky if you even make it to the end. And if chaos demons truly did have a hand in creating Meg, there are an untold number of other issues you could run into that we can't possibly foresee. They might be able to control her, for example. Turn her against you, or against herself, since they don't actually want the Titans released."

"Then how do we set ourselves up to get to the finish line?" I asked.

"I don't know," said Death. His jaw worked side to side, agitated that he was out of his depth. I couldn't imagine how difficult this was for him. He was the embodiment of one of the two guarantees in life, and he was dealing with something he didn't understand.

"I'll send you with what protections I can, reach out to whatever allies I have in those realms and ask them to provide you with a bit more security, clear the way if they can. But we should just plan out the best path to take, and maybe an alternate, then hope that it's possible to stick to it."

I looked around at my mates. All of them. The thought made my heart beat a bit faster with excitement. We were ready for this, we could do it.

None of us were thrilled about the scenario that we were walking into, but I could see the resoluteness in all of their faces. We would be together, to whatever end.

Death pulled out several rolls of paper, yellowed and crumbling at the edges, spreading them out on the table. "These maps aren't the most up-to-date, but they're close. Not much changes down there." The map on the top was of the fourth realm, the Watcher's territory.

"The entire goal will be to find the closest portal with access to the next realm down. All of these are designed to put travelers to the test to ensure that people can't pass freely up or down. Most of the obstacles you'll come against are mental. Illusions, tricks, hypnosis. Things like that. But there will still be plenty of physical obstacles, and creatures to contend with."

He spread his hands across the map, flattening it. "Just assume automatically that everything wants to kill you. Don't touch anything, stay away from water, don't go in places unless it's unavoidable. Don't talk to anyone, unless they speak to you first, and even then be wary. Nobody will help you. It's all part of an evaluation. Any creature you come across will be working at the behest of the ruler of that realm. And their control over their lands is complete and total. Nothing happens without their awareness. You can't sneak through, you won't get around an obstacle unless they want you to. If they don't like what they see, they will not allow you to pass into the next realm."

"What do they care if we're heading toward more danger?" Remi asked.

Death shook his head. "In this case, it's about protecting you from yourselves, and protecting the realm you're about to enter from any shenanigans you might bring with you. Believe it or not, these are all very delicate ecosystems. Someone coming in and causing a ruckus is bad for everybody. One small change could have a catastrophic effect on all the other realms."

"Knock down one domino, and all the others fall," I said.

"Precisely. These realms were designed as schools, hospitals, rehabilitation centers. The act of living is a messy one, and people need several tries before they get it right. Trauma needs to be healed. Patterns need to be eradicated. Before anyone can be resurrected, they need to be prepared for the next go 'round. The only realm that was designed to be a prison is the seventh. That of the Forsaken. The utterly irredeemable souls that can't be fixed, when biding their time won't learn them any lessons.

They have been cut off from the great resurrection machine in the sky."

"And Tartarus?" asked Andrus.

"Completely separate," said Death. "Belsioch created that realm himself, with help of course. That desperate forlorn energy of the forsaken is what fuels it, but they aren't connected in the same way that the seven realms are to each other. Tartarus was never meant to be a long-term solution, so keep that in mind."

"How could that help us?" Andrus asked.

"Not sure. Just something to think about."

There was a heavy silence before Death cleared his throat and turned back to the map. "The Watcher's realm is largely an open, flat plane. You'll find several watchtowers, maybe some geographical formations. Rivers. I'm not sure what kind of beings he may have residing there now. He was a solitary fellow, but started collecting a menagerie." He spread his hands. "There's no telling what it's extended to."

He pointed to a long line running across the entire length of the map. "I'm going to set you down by this river. Follow it and keep it to your left. The portal lies somewhere in this region, but you'll never find the exact location. The Watcher will find you long before that point."

"And then?" Remi asked.

Death blinked and spoke, deadpan. "And then you hope that he doesn't squash you like a bug. He will judge you; pass that judgment, and if you are worthy in his estimation you'll find yourselves in the fifth realm."

He switched the maps to the one below it.

"There's not really anything there," I said, looking at the mostly blank page with a few scribbles and lines.

"This is Shadow." His mouth pressed into a grim line. "Home to the crazed, fractured souls. The ones that died violent deaths, suffered from grievous injustices that were never resolved in life, were born broken, or were shattered by evil they were unlucky enough to cross paths with."

You could've heard a pin drop in the silence. My skin crawled, thinking about the kind of suffering in that place.

"If Hell is the workhouse where people pay off their karmic debts, and Hekate's realm is where souls learn the lesson they need to level up, this is the trauma ward. None of the souls you'll find here are responsible for their actions. They are there solely to scream until they rid themselves of the pain. Were they can howl every ounce of their fury and the universe will hear all of it where before, their pain always fell on deaf ears. And when they have finally spoken their peace, they will move on."

Death reached behind him to a bag sitting on the sideboard and pulled it to him, dumping its contents on the table.

"Earplugs?" I asked, looking at the bright orange foam nubs.

"Enchanted, but yes. You will be tempted to listen, but it is important that you don't. If you listen, you will share in their pain and not only will that jeopardize you, but it will jeopardize them as well. Taking even a bit of that knowledge with you will slow their progress. These will ensure that you can't hear their cries."

"And people think you don't have a heart," said Felix, trying to lighten the mood.

Death shot it down quick while handing us each a pair. "My number one concern has always been the dead. My job is to care for the immortal souls, not who they are in any one of their lives."

Chastised, Felix sank back into his chair after pocketing his earplugs.

"To find the portal in this realm, you'll have to look for the light. The ruler of Shadow isn't a person as much as the sentience of the realm itself. As you pass through, it too will be judging you. Eventually, you will see a light in the distance and that will be your way out."

He turned the page again. The map below was crowded with information. Waterways, rock formations, every field and plane had a name.

"Hekate's Gate." Death looked at the map almost wistfully. "I would say that this should be your easiest voyage, but it also has the potential to be the most dangerous. Lady Hekate is a force, equal to life and death. Do not think that because of your Titan heritage, that that will endear you to her. She evaluates everybody as a collection of what you have done and what you have the potential to do. She suffers no fools, and if you think you're going to be cheeky with her, you better make it good. Otherwise, the consequences you may suffer as punishment would far outweigh anything I would do." He glared at Felix, who had the sense to look abashed.

"Once you arrive here, a path will appear to you. Take it. Do not stray from it. As long as intermittent torches appear along the way, you're fine. If at any point you stray into darkness, go back. If the darkness surrounds you, call out to Hekate and hope that she answers you. Otherwise, she already made her determination, and you aren't going any farther." He grimaced. "Nor are you going back."

"Any pointers?" Andrus asked.

Death chewed on his lip. "Don't fuck up."

"Cool," Andrus said.

"I will send word ahead to her, as well as to the Watcher. That may grant you a bit of grace, but do not count on it."

He switched maps to the one on the bottom of the stack. "I've already told you about the Forsaken." He reached for a box on the side table behind him and opened it, revealing seven necklaces with simple silver squares etched with sigils.

"These are general protection, but they pack a punch. They should help you the entire way through, but they are geared toward the darker energies you will run into in the seventh realm."

I pointed out the lack of map of Tartarus.

"You've already been there, you don't need me to tell you the way," said Death, rolling up the other maps. "There's a big gate, can't miss it." His humor faded. "What you do when you get there is your call."

Having it all laid out before us didn't make this easier to wrap my mind around. It still seemed surreal. This was finally happening, a journey through the seven realms of hell to jailbreak the Titans.

And after I had done a complete one-eighty and changed my mind about them, knowing they were so quick to push the button that could lead to my end brought back every ounce of conflict I felt. And I knew my mates felt the same.

"What do we do?" I asked. "What do we do... if releasing them is a mistake?"

I thought the question would shock my companions, but I was wrong. Relief surged through the bond, that somebody had said what we were all thinking.

Death nodded his head slowly. "Yes, well. I'm afraid we don't have much choice. Even if their motives aren't what we thought they were, releasing them is still preferable to allowing that Hexengate to open."

"Which could very well be what they were planning the whole time?" I asked. "What if this was all a long game? A very, very long game."

Death's shoulders slumped. "Then we deal with it, however we can. We managed to fight off the Ancients when they were released, at least a few of them. They were far more powerful than the Titans." He tried to summon a confident smile but couldn't quite pull it off. "We'll manage."

He stood from the table. "Now take some time to prepare, do whatever needs to be done, settle any open scores. You leave tonight."

CHAPTER EIGHTEEN

Arthur

"Everybody ready?" Death asked.

"What kind of question is that?" Felix retorted.

"Just trying to keep things polite," said Death, trying to hide the smile on his face. Despite the harsh stance he seemed to take against all contrary attitudes, the man appreciated cheekiness.

"I did attempt to send word to the Watcher, but I can't guarantee he received it." Under his breath, Death added, "Or that he cares."

Losing Sasha was still foremost in my mind, but being bonded with Meg did make this easier. I hadn't expected to take to it like I had. I'd seen it as a necessity, but now that the process was complete, I found I felt a lot less alone. She was grieving as well, and now I knew with certainty that her intentions were always in the best interest of all of us. There was a reason she and Sasha had got along so well, and why Sasha didn't hesitate to give us her blessing.

As we stood there now, I could feel the collective nerves of the group. None of us knew what to expect. Hadi had a brief encounter with the Watcher before, and we've been able to see him through Hadi's memory, but we were physically going to be traversing through the lower realms of the underworld, the most dangerous ones that most people never returned from. And if they did, they weren't the same.

I knew deep down that no matter how much I wanted to think I was prepared for what we were about to face, once we were actually in it, every ounce of my strength and bravery would be tested.

Death locked eyes with each one of us before he drew up the portal. It yawned open on a black abyss, not even a hint of what lay behind it. "Do be careful," he said, giving us a sharp nod. "I'd better see all of you on the other side." He grinned. "We do have a deal, after all."

We all exchanged glances to see who would go first, but Meg beat us all to it. She stepped forward, head held high and shoulders set, before walking through.

Death chuckled. "What are the rest of you waiting for?"

One by one, we crossed over that threshold into the unknown. I kept my fingers crossed, hands firmly at my sides as I took one last look around at the world I was familiar with.

And when I opened my eyes...

We stood in the middle of a vast expanse. The air was hot, and close, every breath thick. My lungs felt tight as I struggled with the sudden change. All my companions had made it through, and we stood arrayed behind Meg.

A river flowed a few hundred yards away, the water placid but lit from underneath with an eerie red glow, like a fire burning low to embers. There was no ceiling over our heads, but what seemed like a vast expanse of dark sky.

The ground underneath our feet was a hard shale, and the edges of the river dropped off sharply like the channel had been dug out by hand, cut along the banks in a perfectly straight line.

Great towers made of dark rock stood intermittently across the plane, so tall, the spires at their tips seemed like they would puncture the darkness. There had to be at least a dozen of them in sight, and shapes far in the distance that looked like more of the same.

"There are shadows everywhere," said Remi.

"What kind of shadows?" Gareth asked.

Remi shook his head, his wings shuddering in discomfort. "They don't have much of a form. They're tall and thin. Some of them have mouths—"

"With bright white teeth," Meg finished.

Remi nodded. "Do you know what they are?"

Meg shook her head. "No. I've never seen this before."

Remi elaborated. "They don't seem to have any interest in us."

"I suppose we should forge ahead," said Meg, but she made no move to do so. Her hair was bound tightly in a braid, which was coiled at the nape of her neck, and the loose leather pants and corset she wore seemed like armor as she stood, the general of a fierce army.

She tightened the laces on her leather bracers and checked that all her weapons were in place while we did the same. Hadi and Gareth were the most lightly armed, preferring to run light and take full advantage of their own natural weaponry.

Felix and I were the opposite, with swords, knives, and bows. Andrus carried double short swords and Remi preferred axes, which was a change for him, although a polearm would've been impractical.

Meg carried an axe on each hip, a sword at her back, and a knife at each ankle, and she glowed with power. It was still a blinding sight, one that nothing could prepare you for. Our enemies would quake in her presence. She was the embodiment of everything that made the Titans mighty, packed into the frame of a small human.

She looked around at us. "Any last words?" she joked. "I feel like I should give a gladiator send-off."

"We who are about to die, salute you," I said.

"Who's the Emperor in this situation?" asked Felix. "I've always fancied that position for myself."

I just rolled my eyes and Andrus and Remi groaned. In the past, I would've taken those words a lot more seriously. Felix had always had enough... confidence? ...to inspire an entire army to victory. But I'd noticed a significant change in him.

He was a better man for it. I always knew I could trust him at my back, but now I knew that he was in it for far less selfish reasons.

Meg led the way forward. When we planned this out with Death, he had advised us to follow the river's edge, but not to go in the water at all costs. Most of the waters that we would encounter were benign, but some would be instant death, and others were no less malicious, but far more mysterious in their effect.

"Remember, don't touch the water, don't go near the towers, and if you feel like you're being watched, don't look behind you," Hadi said.

"How far did you have to travel last time before you met him?" I asked. I didn't have a problem with the rules, except for the one that said I shouldn't look behind me. I always had a problem fighting impulses like that, and being told not to do it... I didn't like my chances.

Hadi shrugged one shoulder. "It's hard to say. It could've been hours, or it could've been days. You lose track of time very quickly here."

"Great," said Meg. She forced a smile when she could sense all our concern. I admired the brave face she attempted to put on, but there was no use hiding the stress she was under. At any moment she could blink out of existence.

"We'll make it through this," I said, squeezing her shoulder. She placed her hand over mine and ran her thumb over the back of my hand, nodding.

"Yes, we will," she said, determination setting in her features.

It was impossible to get the full scope of the vastness of this place. As we traveled, we tried to keep conversation light, even talked about our ideas for the future as we would finally be able to build lives together. I very much hoped that we would all make it to the end of this. These men were already family to me, and Meg was quickly becoming a focal point in my ideas of moving on.

We traveled in silence, keeping watch and straining all our senses to hopefully catch a threat before it got anywhere near us.

I was watching the towers in the distance when one of them caught my eye. There were lights on in some of the windows. This tower looked identical to the others. Dark smooth stone, no sign of seams anywhere, like it had grown out of the ground like that. The base of each one was hexagonal, several hundred yards wide at least. Each edge was so sharp and perfectly straight, it would've been an architectural miracle if it had been built anywhere else but here.

A faint humming issued from all of them as you got close, like it could sense your presence and was ready to react if you got within a certain radius. The energy that emanated from all of them made my skin crawl.

"Do you see those?" I asked, motioning ahead. The windows looked almost like portholes dotting the face of the tower.

"Lanterns?" Remi asked.

"Do you think there are actually people in there?" asked Felix.

Hadi was staring at the tower with intense concentration. "I don't like it," he said. "Give it a wide berth."

Just then, a chorus of shrieks sounded behind us. Every one of us froze, barely resisting the urge to look back.

"Fuck, fuck, fuck," said Meg, trying to keep her breathing even. Her stance was so rigid as she fought the instinct to turn, all her muscles must've been seizing.

"Run!" Hadi shouted, and we wasted no time following that order. We raced across the plane, the shrieks following close behind, never getting nearer, but we never lost them either.

Andrus tripped and went sprawling onto the ground and the shrieks sounded so close this time that he flipped around and looked back.

CHAPTER NINETEEN

Meg

Everything seemed to move in slow motion. Andrus fell, those horrible cries sounded so close, and he looked back. Before the warning was even out of my mouth, his whole body spasmed and his soul... left. It pulled away from his prone body, and I ran over to him, kneeling at his head, crushing my eyes closed, and blindly facing the threat coming at us.

My mates walked backward, positioning themselves by Andrus's feet so they could watch us without being equally tempted to turn.

I reached for his soul, wrapping my power around him like a lasso and pulling him back. Whatever force caused him to leave his body wrenched him away from me again. I felt around until my hands landed on Andrus's shoulders. His body was already getting cold.

I tapped into my mates' power as well as digging deep into my own, gathering my strength before giving one vicious tug, and freeing Andrus's soul. He shot back into his body, and I heard him gasp.

The force I'd used to pull him snapped back into me, like a cable tie at maximum tension broke and pelted toward me with frightening speed. I bit back a cry as Andrus's power overwhelmed me, flooding into my body like it was my own.

I had to get rid of it, it was too much, but I couldn't just fling it away. That might kill Andrus. Hadi took my face in his hands and turned it gently toward him. Still not opening my eyes, I felt his own power mingle with mine, guiding it with what to do.

Together, we severed the connection, but it was still overwhelming my system.

Use it as an attack, he said. *Let it go.*

I imagined all of it coalescing into one giant ball of energy, and I did just that, flinging the entirety away from me. I could see the resulting blast of light through my closed eyelids, my mates stumbling from the resulting shockwave.

Everything went silent. Slowly, I opened my eyes, the deep brown of Hadi's the first thing I saw. He helped me stand and I kept my eyes locked on him the entire time. Andrus stirred, groaning. Hadi turned his attention to the vampire and did the same, ensuring he was steady on his feet before stepping away.

"What just happened?" Felix asked.

I blew out a breath. "Damned if I know."

"Bad choice of words," Andrus said, still clearly shaken but smiling.

The only one that didn't seem to be in a celebratory mood was Arthur. He stared ahead, lost in thought. "Arthur?" I asked.

He blinked and met my eyes. "What did you do just now? To get Andrus back?"

I tried to think of the best way to put it into words. "Just kind of roped him with my power and pulled. Really hard." My brow furrowed. "Why?"

"Your signature changed," he said, brow equally creased in confusion.

"My—what?" I must've misheard him.

"Your signature. It changed," he said.

"Is that possible?" Gareth asked. "Are you sure it wasn't something else?"

Arthur shook his head. "Absolutely. I'm positive that her signature changed."

"What did it feel like?" I asked. I'd been too distracted dealing with everything else. Maybe he was onto something.

"At first, it was a blend. You and Andrus in the same body. But then it morphed. Changed into something entirely new. Now it's back to normal."

I was speechless. I wanted to ask him again if he was positive just out of my own shock, but I wouldn't do him that disservice.

We all took a minute to let it sink in. "That's our answer," I said.

The bond hummed with excited energy. If I could change my signature, but still maintain my power and all the Titan's signatures within it, I could open the gate.

But there was no time to celebrate. A great booming laugh that promised danger sounded across the plane, coming from all directions, right before a massive figure materialized in front of us.

The Watcher.

Being told that a creature has a thousand eyes and actually seeing it are two very different things. You can never fully comprehend the horror of it. There were eyes all over its body, blinking with different shapes and colors, round and slit pupils, some just glowing solid red. There were arms and legs, but the torso and neck and head all ran together in some kind of gelatinous blob. The mouth was just a slit across its face that opened into a toothless dark with a lolling gray tongue.

"You come to my realm and make such a mess?"

His voice boomed down around us, blasting through my body like the bass at a concert, interrupting my heartbeat with the force of it.

What did he mean, mess? I looked around and realized with a sinking sensation that several of the towers had crumbled when I'd sent out that blast of excess energy.

"Forgive me, that wasn't my intention," I said. "There were things. Chasing us."

"I have no idea what you're talking about," the Watcher said. "Any intentions don't matter as much as"—he looked at the destruction—"actions."

Shit. We were only a few hours in, and it looked like our journey was going to be cut short.

"Did you really like those towers anyway?" Felix asked.

All of us froze and turned to stare at him. I shook my head subtly, hoping he would get the hint.

"What?" the giant boomed.

"Seems like this place is in need of a remodel. You can do better," he said.

I closed my eyes, preparing to get squished underfoot.

Instead, the Watcher chuckled with genuine mirth. The chuckle gave away to a laugh, belly-shaking, the ground trembling under our feet.

When the Watcher's laughter petered off, a thousand eyes stared down at us. "I suppose I could. There are much easier ways to knock down a building, however. Ones that aren't quite so messy. Or loud."

Felix bowed at the waist. "It won't happen again." He straightened. "Unless you have need for a demolition crew."

The Watcher rumbled. "Don't push your luck, elf."

Felix bowed again and moved to the back of the group.

"I know of your mission," said the Watcher. "And while I may have decided to let you pass through my realm, you won't make it to the end as you are."

"How so?" Gareth asked.

"My job is to observe, not to guide. You'll have to find those answers on your own."

My hand shot out to cover Felix's mouth before he could say something that would get us all killed. I could've sworn several of the Watcher's eyes winked at me when I did.

"Is there anything you can tell us? Of what you've seen of our path ahead?" asked Hadi.

The Watcher's eyes all blinked in unison as they looked at the dragon. "I've met you before," he said.

Hadi bowed low. "Yes, my lord. You told me where I could find Osiris."

The Watcher nodded. "Yes, yes. I did, didn't I? And did that errand prove fruitful for you?"

"It didn't have the outcome I wished for, but it was enlightening, nevertheless."

Another nod, the creature's bulbous neck wobbling. I'd seen Jell-O molds with less wiggle. "Very good. I'm glad you used the experience wisely."

Two slits where a nose would've been widened as the creature inhaled deeply. "Very well. You may pass." He motioned with his right hand and the world seemed to buckle and warp as from a great distance a shape came zooming toward us. It was the portal, active and inviting us to step through.

His eyes gave one final wink, and he disappeared.

"Why did you slap your hand over my mouth?" Felix asked, trying to look hurt. "I wasn't going to say anything."

I sighed and shook my head. "I'll believe that about the same time a yellow brick road appears to usher us safely to a land of gumdrops and candy canes called Tartarus."

We fished our earplugs out of our pockets. As soon as I put them in, all sound was cut off.

Ready? I asked.

After a round of affirmatives, I braced myself and stepped through.

CHAPTER TWENTY

Gareth

After the boiling heat of the Watcher's realm, the icy cold of this one went bone deep. The shock of it took my breath and made gooseflesh rise painfully on my arms.

The air felt like it was buzzing against my skin, waves of electricity washing over and through me. I pressed my earplugs in tighter, just in case, the vibrations hitting me there the hardest.

All around us was black smoke, undulating in time with the waves of vibration. I could barely see five feet ahead.

Are those sound waves? Andrus asked. *Is that what I'm feeling?*

That makes sense, said Meg, shivering. She looked around and waved her hand through the smoke, trying to clear it. *Can any of you see anything?*

No, said Arthur. *What is this? Some kind of fog?*

Shrouds, said Remi. *These are souls.*

A note of shock emanated from Meg. She reached out again, leaving her hand in the air, palm up. As we watched, slim, shadowy fingers reached out, tapping her hand, almost like they were testing to see if it was real. Then the shadow rested its hand in Meg's.

She looked at us and I could feel her devastation, if her face hadn't said it all already. She gently pulled her hand away from the spirit's and she spoke a few words of blessing under her breath. *Find peace.* Death said we couldn't listen to them, but he said nothing about wishing them well.

It was slow going, trying to see through the swirling masses and not make any missteps. If Remi hadn't had wings, we would've lost him down a crevasse that split across our path. He and Hadi took the lead after that. Meg tried to conjure her wings, but it didn't work.

Even though we couldn't hear the words being said, the constant buffering of the cacophony was wearing on me. We'd come to a patch of land that had sparse grass instead of hard stone, but it looked like a lush bed of moss to my tired body.

How much longer do you think we can do this? I asked. *I'm about ready to drop.*

I feel the same, said Felix. *Can we stop?*

Meg leaned forward and braced herself on her knees, breathing heavily. Her and Remi were taking the brunt of the effects. As the mediums in the group, they were lit up like beacons to the dead. The entire journey so far, they'd been dodging and shrugging off grasping hands. Meg was saying constant *mea culpas*, and it was killing her not to be able to help.

Death didn't say anything about it not being safe to stop, she said. *But I'm not sure how restful it'll be if we're still being bombarded.*

I can shield us, for a little while at least, said Hadi.

Are you sure? Andrus asked. *Doesn't that take a lot of energy for you to sustain?*

It's just for a little while. I won't push it. Hadi closed his eyes in concentration and called up a golden orb of power, expanding it so we were all encompassed inside it. The constant push and pull of the wails ceased and it was finally still. The dragon sat, legs crossed, eyes still closed as he focused.

Meg didn't need to be offered twice. She sat down and Remi joined her, pulling her into his chest where she fell asleep immediately. He followed shorty after.

Go ahead, said Arthur. *I'll keep watch. I seem to be the least affected out of all of you.*

They find you as boring as we do, teased Felix.

Arthur ignored him and took up a seat across from Hadi on the other side of the bubble.

My eyelids drew down heavily, and I was out.

Andrus woke me, punching my arm repeatedly until I opened my eyes. *Let's go, sleeping beauty.*

At least beauty sleep does something for me, you goblin, I said, smirking.

Hadi dropped the barrier once we were all awake, looking a bit sweaty but otherwise no worse for wear. We continued our trek, keeping our eyes peeled for any sign of the light that would indicate the portal was close, but I was starting to lose hope. We couldn't see anything outside of our immediate surroundings, how could we expect to find a guiding light?

Meg stumbled, going down heavily on one knee. *I'm fine. I tripped.*

Like hell you did, said Felix, helping her up. *You can either be carried or ride piggyback. Choose.*

She was about to refuse both but relented when she saw that none of us believed her "tripping" excuse. *Piggyback then,* she said.

Felix bent down so she could wrap her arms around his shoulders before hoisting her up. She rested her chin on his shoulder and fell asleep again. I caught the happy grin on his face before he saw me looking and tried to hide it.

Remi was clearly dragging, too. *I'd offer to carry you, but you're a bit much for me. Sorry,* I said.

He laughed, but the strain of staying on his feet was obvious.

I can offer you a shoulder, though, I said, standing next to him.

Remi looked at me, grateful, before slinging his arm around my shoulder. *Do you think we're close?* he asked.

Gods, I hope so.

But we weren't.

The next time we stopped, it was Felix who attempted to put up a barrier. Hadi couldn't maintain his half-shifted form anymore and expending any more energy could be dangerous. Felix's abilities with that brand of magick were lacking, but it was more than the rest of us could do and it gave us a small reprieve.

When we set off again, Meg made it less than half the time before she began to flag. Andrus didn't even ask, just offered his shoulders and she climbed on. *I'm sorry,* she said, before falling asleep. Remi sagged against Arthur's shoulder, each step a stumbling struggle. We couldn't afford to give either of them any more of our energy.

We all exchanged worried glances. If we didn't get out of here soon...

What if Hadi tries a fly over? suggested Arthur.

I already tried to shift, said Hadi. His frustration was evident, even without the emotion that flared through the bond. *I can't manage it.*

So that also means fire is out? Felix asked.

Hadi nodded. *I could summon it if necessary, but only as a last resort. If we need another barrier—*

The rest of what he said didn't register. Meg, being carried in front of me, still had her eyes shut tight, but I could just see two spectral hands trying to work the earplugs out of her ears. It already had one halfway out when I stumbled forward and clapped my hands over her ears.

The spirits are trying to sabotage her! I said. They all stopped, and Remi clapped his hands to his own ears.

Me too, he said, almost falling. The dark shrouds crowded in around him and Meg, long fingers poking and pulling. Before we could formulate a plan, I felt my own earplugs wrenched out.

Gareth! Hadi lunged forward, trying to retrieve them, but it was too late. I watched them carried off by a spirit as the tumultuous noise overwhelmed me. My vision blurred and a sharp pain in both ears made me cry out. Warm liquid ran down both sides of my face and when I investigated, I found blood. Even though my eardrums had ruptured the sound was still unrelenting, a cacophony of wailing with barely audible words.

I sank to my knees, dropping my hands from Meg's ears, and through vision going dark around the edges, her first earplug popped out.

And then I knew nothing.

Blurred shapes.

Frantic bursts of conversation as my companions spoke back and forth.

A golden sheen over everything.

Slowly, I came back to myself to realize the world around me was in even more chaos than when I passed out.

Hadi had constructed individual barriers around each of our heads which kept the spirits away from the earplugs, but it did not prevent them from attacking us outright.

Meg and Remi were both lying unconscious while Felix and Arthur vainly attempted to defend us with weapons. All they succeeded in doing was cutting through wisps of smoke before the figures would reincorporate and attack again.

I did a double take when I saw Andrus. He had unleashed the full force of his demonic Nosmortem power. His face had elongated to make room for tiger-like jaws. He was taller, leaner, his long arms ending in sharply clawed hands as he swiped at any spirit that got too near. Green flame danced off his fingers, the only thing that was having any effect against the ravenous souls.

Hadi encased himself in a barrier so he could maintain focus while trying to protect the rest of us, but they were attacking it on all sides, throwing themselves against it. It would only be a matter of time before it broke.

Head still pounding, I stood, drawing my sword. It clearly wouldn't do any good, but it was all I had to contribute against this type of enemy.

A loud crack in the distance made me look around. High above us, I could just see a light glowing, growing brighter as it descended. The spirit's frenzy reached a peak as the gate lowered itself right in the middle of the melee.

Gareth, grab Meg and go, said Arthur.

I nodded, scooping her up and jumping through the gate. As soon as we landed, I hurried out of the way and the others piled through, Felix with Remi slung over his shoulder, Hadi at the rear. The second he was through, the gate snapped shut.

CHAPTER TWENTY-ONE

Felix

As soon as I dragged the gargoyle's lazy ass through the gate, I dumped him on the ground next to Meg, still unconscious. His wing caught me in the face on the way down and I cursed.

"That's what I get for being nice," I said, rubbing the spot on my cheek where those oddly velvety wings had brushed my skin. Creepy.

I crouched down next to Meg and pulled out her remaining earplug, touching my fingers to her neck to check for her pulse. Steady, just like her breathing. She was lucky Hadi had been so quick with those personal barriers. He'd gotten it around her head right before the plug popped out all the way.

"I'm pretty sure she's sleeping," I said.

Hadi bent down to confirm. "Yes," he said, shoving his own earplugs back in his pocket.

Arthur cocked his head. "We're not going to have to go back through this way to get out, right?"

We all shared ominous looks. "Even if the Titans have gone bad, I'd rather hitch a ride with them than go back through that," said Andrus.

The portal had opened out on a cliff. Angry waters raged below, the spray misting my face as I peered down. On the opposite side were thick woods, dense underbrush packed so tight they would be impassable.

Death had said we were to wait until a path appeared. I looked around nervously. Was she watching us right now? Lady Hekate?

The night sky overhead was full of stars and a comet went streaking by. Those other realms could learn a few things from this one.

"Are you feeling alright?" Hadi asked Gareth. I blinked. I'd already forgotten he was exposed to the voices.

Twin lines of blood leaked out either ear and he looked haggard, like he hadn't slept in weeks or eaten in a month.

He shook his head. "I don't know." He stared down at Meg before sitting heavily beside her. "My eardrums healed, but I feel strange. Can't say how. I couldn't actually understand any of the words, except maybe one or two, probably not even from the same person. It was just a wall of noise."

"Make sure you say something if you sense a change," said Hadi, clapping Gareth on the shoulder.

"We should all get some rest while we can. We can't go anywhere until these two wake up anyway. I'll take first watch," said Andrus.

Gareth shifted to his wolf form—he'd heal faster that way—and lay down beside Meg. Her fingers curled ever so slightly into his fur. The grass was lush and as I lay down at Meg's feet, I was instantly asleep.

When I dreamed it was of a tall, refined woman with wavy black hair to her waist. Her olive skin was flawless, and her brow was furrowed over fathomless brown eyes, flecked with gold. All it took was meeting her gaze and I knew instantly that she had read all my secrets, knew me better than I knew myself.

Her full lips curved into a smile, but it gave nothing away of what conclusion she'd come to.

"You've already begun your inward journey, I see," she said, canting her head to the side. "What have you learned so far?"

"I—" I was too intimidated to speak. This woman was power, and fury, and knowledge, wisdom... the embodiment of magick. A being that survived without the need for, or concern of time, for the only thing that mattered to her was what she could see and judge in the moment.

Hekate.

Around her stood three black dogs, standing about knee height. They didn't growl or make any sign that they cared for my presence one way or the other.

As she watched me, she placed her hand on one of the dog's heads and it looked up at its mistress in adoration.

"Go on," she encouraged, her face still lacking identifiable emotion.

I shrugged. "I'm an asshole."

She stilled before letting out a surprised laugh. It was only then that I remembered Death's warning about being cheeky with her.

"And do you take umbrage with that realization?" she asked.

I considered my answer carefully. "Partly. I regret the harm that I put my friends in. I'm ashamed of some of my past actions. But as for overall attitude"—I splayed my hands—"I can't say I plan to change all that much."

Then she was gone.

I woke with a start as Andrus shook my shoulder. "Sorry," he said. "You were the first one asleep, so I figured I'd wake you up for next watch."

"How kind of you," I said, getting up and stretching with a long groan.

Andrus took my place on the pre-warmed grass, and I sat in the most uncomfortable position I could. I hadn't noticed before how many crickets there were. Far in the distance, thunder rumbled, and I hoped we wouldn't get caught in the rain.

Had that dream been a visitation? And if it was, had I passed judgment? Things like that never really mattered to me before. I was a spoiled brat who grew into a spoiled man. The only reason I devoted myself to the Titans was for the adventure. And maybe the glory.

I did care deeply for my friends, and I was noticing significant changes in myself. But what if I had been found unworthy?

My gaze drifted to Meg and the first inklings of worry roiled in my gut. Would that doom me? Cut me off from the others? From her?

I wanted to be worthy of her. That was a realization I'd been slowly coming around to. Every confession I'd made to her since they returned from the underworld had been true. But it went deeper than that, now. I was discovering things I'd never allowed myself to admit.

I wasn't clinging tightly to my playboy ways, but the thought of *that kind* of devotion was a lot for me to accept. In the court of the Unseelie, it would be a weakness that would likely get both of us killed. Not for vengeance, or out of jealousy. Those were for chumps.

No. Any dark fae who showed a desire for *love* would be hunted down for sport.

I chuckled to myself. What kind of poor sot was I turning into? First allowing myself empathy, and now falling over myself to earn the trust of a woman I very possibly might love? A woman who by all means should've cut me out back at Farah's house. I'd slapped her ass like she was nothing more than a servant tending to a corpulent pig of a noble.

That man was a joke. I could be better, or at least I'd try.

For her.

Chapter Twenty-Two

Andrus

I may have woken Felix up a bit early, but I was dragging. Everything hurt. Taking my full form was always taxing, and every time I struck out at one of the spirits, it took more energy than it should have if I had been keeping up on training.

Meg's feet dipped toward me as I lay down. She was still asleep, but I could imagine her toes stretching and curling in her thick boots. Her feet usually ended up tucked against mine when she was cold. Gareth was shivering, his eyes cracked open enough for me to see his eyes rolling wildly in his head. It was at least thirty seconds of exposure before Hadi had managed to get the bubble shield around his head. I shuddered at the thought of being blasted with that much agony.

As soon as my head hit the cushy grass, I was out.

And I was back on the streets of Babylon. A young man, barely even a hundred years old. Just coming into my demonic abilities, the vampiric side was harder to control. My mother hadn't had time to teach me anything before my father forced her out.

There were so many cravings. All I could think about was blood, the iron tang of it, the hot gush as the geyser burst. I'd been hunting this quarter of the city for weeks, taking at least one victim a night. What did it matter? They were poor anyway. A quick death would be better than whatever their daily lives would bring to them.

Tonight I had my sights on a thief that thought he was really something. To his credit, he had been gaining quite a reputation for making it past even the wealthiest landowners' security to steal from their coffers. But his reign would end tonight.

The man was right in front of me now, just a few paces away. He had no idea I was here. I sneered. The fool deserved to die.

A woman melted out of the shadows, stepping between me and my quarry. Her long, dark hair framed a strong face that was staring at me with pity.

"For a father to turn his own son into a killer," she said.

I was taken aback. Who was this woman? And why did she speak like she knew me?

"There are better ways to sate your thirst, are there not?"

"What's it to you?" I asked.

Her eyebrows rose. "Everything."

I stood up a little straighter at her answer. It wasn't what I was expecting to hear, and it made a big impression.

"There's nothing wrong with this," I said, defiant.

She stared at me, unblinking, saying nothing.

"These people are dregs. They're worthless."

Still no reply. I was getting agitated, and if she wasn't careful—

The thief disappeared around the corner and I swore. "Now look what you've done," I hissed, moving to go around her.

I slammed backward into the wall behind me, the air whooshing out of my lungs as the stone cracked. Without taking a step she was in front of me somehow, leaning down to peer into my face.

"Andrus," she said, her voice calm, completely unconcerned about the confrontation she had begun.

"What?" I growled, struggling to get free. Some force was pinning me there.

"Andrus," she said again.

My head swam and everything went fuzzy. "What?" I asked, confused this time. Where was I? Was this Babylon? None of us have been able to time travel like Meg, but I felt a rush of pride that I might've been the first. No idea why I would've chosen to come here though.

"Andrus," the woman said again, recapturing my attention.

Three black dogs melted out of the shadows and arranged themselves around her feet.

She smiled, no real emotion in it of any kind. "How does it feel to be back home?"

Oh, shit. This was her. Lady Hekate.

"This was never my home, Lady," I said, careful to keep my tone respectful.

"Perhaps not," she conceded. "More of a hunting ground, then?"

"No, Lady." I couldn't meet her eye.

"Andrus," she said, tone chastising.

She knew I was lying, but I've never been that good at it to begin with. Stealing, yes. Only by necessity. Lying…

"It was a different time. I was a different man," I said.

"Not so different," she said, tilting her head to the side.

"Worlds different," I insisted.

"You don't hesitate to kill, even now."

"I do. It's never wanton. It's always necessary. To protect the people I care about."

The look on her face became knowing. "You're not such a saint, as you would like people to believe."

"What people assume, and what I assert are two different things. I never claimed to be one. I just try to be a good man, and do right by people."

"Now," said Hekate. "It hasn't always been that way."

"Has anybody lived a life they were one hundred percent proud of?" I asked. "We all make mistakes."

"Quite the mistake." She motioned behind her and a strangled cry lodged in my throat. Piles of bodies were stacked, almost as tall as the buildings around them. Hundreds, maybe thousands, in various states of decay.

"Was each one of these a mistake?"

I stared at those piles for a long time before I answered. "No."

"Then why did you do it?"

"I was hungry. And angry. And lost. And these people paid the price for it."

She nodded her head slowly, encouraging me to go on.

"I drowned my pain in blood. I'm not proud of it, but it can't be undone."

"Then why haven't you shared this with anyone?"

"Shame," I said.

"Your companions all have darkness in their pasts. Do you think they would judge you harshly?" One of the dogs at her feet yawned and I had the absurd notion to ask if I was boring it.

"It doesn't matter if they do or not. I judge myself harshly. Those things are better left buried."

"Things?" Her mouth pulled into a frown. "These were lives, not things."

My stomach sank all the way to my feet and my breathing became shallow as my mind raced. My mouth gaped open, flapping uselessly as I tried to form words.

The bodies begin to move, the piles writhing like maggot-infested meat. I really hadn't changed at all, had I? This whole time, those people were always nameless and faceless.

"I thought—"

Hekate's face was stone. "You thought what?" Her tone was ice.

"I tried to make amends. I turned my back on my father, on the lifestyle. Broke free from his rules and influence."

"Did you?"

"Yes, I—"

"How do you know?" she asked.

"Because I changed. I gained control of myself. I realized it was wrong."

"What part of it?"

I stared at her. "Part..."

"What did you find wrong?"

"The killing," I said hesitantly, brow knit in confusion.

"Why?" she breathed, inches from my face. Her breath smelled like wine and roses.

"It wasn't necessary. It was wasteful." The confusion evaporated as it was replaced by horror. I'd just referred to the people I'd murdered like they were cattle.

"There it is," she said, leaning away from me.

I sat up with a start to find Meg kneeling in front of me. "Are you alright?" she asked, wiping sweat from my face. "You were talking in your sleep."

"You're awake?" I asked, looking around to make sure I wasn't still in a dream.

"Just."

"Are you okay?"

She laughed. "You still haven't answered that same question."

I sat back. "I'm fine." The guilt of lying immediately ate at me, something I'm pretty sure wasn't only my conscience at work. "Lady Hekate paid me a visit in my dream. She doesn't mess around with those lessons of hers."

"No, she does not," said Felix. "She came for me earlier."

"I wonder who else has had a run-in?" said Meg, looking around. Remi was still asleep, as was Gareth. Arthur was just beginning to wake. Hadi was—

"Where's Hadi?" I asked, staring around as far as the view would allow. Before we could panic too much, his dragon came swooping out of the sky, blowing fire in great gusts.

He roared as he saw us awake—well, probably after he saw Meg was awake—and banked to his left. He was coming in so fast it seemed like he wouldn't be able to slow his descent before he plowed into us. Meg gasped and backed up a step, but I'd seen him do this trick too many times. He transformed right as he hit the cliff's edge and walked gracefully over, crushing Meg to his chest tightly.

"I'm alright," she said, tilting her head up to receive his heated kiss. "I promise," she said, slightly breathless. "Are you?"

"Yes," he said, stroking her cheek. I'd never seen Hadi so worried about someone. She truly had captured his heart.

Welcome to the club.

She looked back behind her at Remi and Gareth as Hadi dressed, a frown creasing her face. "Remi's still asleep, but something about Gareth doesn't seem right."

I frowned, peering closer as Hadi moved to crouch next to him, placing his hand lightly on the wolf's body. That seemed to rouse Gareth, and he shook his shaggy head, rolling back up onto his feet before changing back.

He looked bleary-eyed at the two of the them. "What?"

He stood, despite Meg begging him to wait a minute, and swayed on his feet, Meg and Hadi supporting either side of him.

Hadi shook his head. "You're right. He's getting worse."

"I'm right here, you don't have to talk about me like I'm still asleep," Gareth grumbled.

"Worse?" Meg asked.

I realized Meg had been unconscious when Gareth had been exposed to the Shadows.

"The spirits ripped out his earplugs. He got a full blast of that noise," I said.

Meg looked back at Gareth, horrified. "What? How? That's got to be what's causing this, right? What do we do?"

Gareth pushed away from both of them and stood on his own two feet. "It'll be fine. Once we get going. I just need to keep moving."

"Gareth—" Meg attempted to stop him, but he cut her off, grabbing his clothes.

"Please, Meg," he said, giving her a tight smile and running his thumb over her bottom lip. "I'll be fine."

There wasn't even a hint that she believed him, but she let it go for now.

"Hey, guys," said Felix. "I think we got to go-ahead to continue."

"Do you see something?" Arthur asked.

Felix pointed to a spot in the trees, about fifty yards down from where we were standing. A path had appeared, where I was certain there wasn't one before.

At the head of it, a torch burned brightly.

CHAPTER TWENTY-THREE

Remi

I woke to the feeling of being carried, one set of hands under each arm as they hauled me to my feet. "What's going on?" I asked, voice thick with sleep.

Arthur and Felix both started. "Gods, man, don't do that," said Felix, forcing a chuckle.

Brain still muddled with sleep, I didn't understand what he was saying. "Don't do what? I just woke up."

He shook his head. "Never mind."

"Where are we going?" I asked as they set me carefully on my feet.

Felix pointed. "The path just appeared. We wanted to get moving just in case." He looked me up and down, suspicious I might keel over. "We didn't know how long you'd be asleep."

"Are you feeling alright?" Arthur asked.

I shrugged. "Exhausted, still. But otherwise I feel fine. I think. All those spirits draining me..." He shook his head. "I didn't expect it to take such a toll."

Meg had walked back to join us from where she'd been speaking with Hadi at the head of the line we'd formed, walking along the wall of trees. The woods made me uneasy. It felt like I was being watched by a hungry predator, stalking us and biding their time.

The roar of the ocean could've easily lulled me back to sleep. I smiled at Meg. "You handled it far better than I did. You don't even look tired."

She placed her hand on my chest and the warm flow of energy she pushed directly into me went to work revitalizing me. "From the sounds of things, you didn't have personal chauffeurs to carry you around while you napped," she said, pulling back when the drag of sleep no longer had me in its grip.

"Thank you," I said, drawing her in for a hug.

"I'm glad you're okay," she said against my chest.

"Let's hope we stay that way," said Felix, staring ahead at the entrance of the path that disappeared quickly with a curve through the thick trees.

Andrus and the others gave me nods of acknowledgment as we joined but I noticed the gray tinge to Gareth's skin that was usually my domain. He shook his head slightly, imploring me not ask.

"We'll have to go single file," said Hadi. "Stick to the center of the trail. I don't trust there's not something hiding in that underbrush."

"And remember to keep an eye out for the torches. If there aren't any ahead, we go back," said Andrus.

"And if there aren't any behind us, kiss your ass goodbye," said Felix.

Meg sighed and the elf chuckled.

Hadi nodded sharply. "Let's go." He took the lead, stepping onto the path, followed by Andrus, Gareth, and Meg, who had taken the central position in the group. It made all of us feel better to have eyes on her and to be a buffer from whatever was ahead, but I'd lay odds she took no notice. She just wanted to keep an eye on Gareth while he tried to push past whatever was ailing him.

I understood not wanting to slow the group down, especially now. But he would be a liability if he let this continue without asking for help. He was clearly suffering far worse than the rest of us. I'd only caught a brief glimpse of him collapsing after his earplugs were stolen before I passed out, but it was enough to see the horrible twisting of his face in pain and the way his body twitched as he hit the ground.

Something had followed him through that gate, but I wasn't adept enough to pull back the curtain of spirit and look at the fine details.

Arthur was behind me and Felix brought up the rear. As soon as my feet hit the path, the closeness of the air became stifling. After the brisk, salt-tinged ocean breeze, this was humid and hot.

Sound became dulled, not only because of the thick carpet of leaves underneath our feet but because of the canopy that closed in so tightly overhead that we couldn't see even a hint of stars.

We walked. Just as the light from one torch would fade, another appeared ahead, guiding our way, and giving us reassurance that we were still welcome. Other than the occasional whisper, none of us spoke, not even mentally, through the bond.

We were surrounded by constant rustling in the trees on either side, like large creatures were stalking us, but that didn't make any sense. As densely packed as the trees were, it shouldn't have been possible for something that big to move. But this was the sixth realm of Hell. Nothing had to make sense here.

I could just hear a light whispering, seeming to come from somebody standing close by, but every time I would look there was no one. We'd all given ourselves at least five feet of space between us, to ease the feeling of claustrophobia.

"You've done the work, suffered through the darkness. I have nothing to teach you."

A woman was standing beside me, and I fell back a couple of paces. I looked around at the others, but they were frozen.

"Don't worry about them," she said. "The ones that haven't gotten their turn already, will."

"What do you want?" She was just as Felix described. He hadn't gone into much detail about his experience, but he made sure to try to prepare us for her presence. No description could've prepared me for how... massive that presence was. She was only a little taller than me, but she had the kind of bearing that the world wasn't big enough to accommodate. It wasn't a sense of ego, but *greatness*.

She smiled, wide enough to showcase the apples of her cheeks. Her voice was low and melodic. "I neither want nor need anything from you." Her words were kind. "You have done the work already."

"Work?" I asked, confused.

She rested her hand on my cheek, and I leaned into the touch full of motherly affection. "Great suffering has befallen you, but it didn't break you. You could have let those years in the dungeons ruin you, but in the end, it only made you more determined to save others from the same fate. You could've turned your back on this mission, on the Titans, on the entire world for the cruelty it's done you. And yet here you are. Dutiful companion, stalwart friend, devoted mate. The only person you ultimately blamed for your suffering was yourself."

She rested both of her hands on my shoulders. "I am here to release you of that burden."

My breath hitched, my pulse racing. "My Lady?"

"Be assured, you are a wonderful example of learning from the pain. You have withstood every test and returned, transformed for the better. I am proud of you, child."

Tears streamed down my face. Was I dreaming?

Another smile. "No. This is all too real. Be absolved of the burdens you carry. I will take them from here."

A glow emanated from her hands, illuminating her face. My chest burned and a ragged gasp tore from my throat as a darkness wrenched free from somewhere deep down. A lightness spread through my body all the way up from my toes. The guilt I'd carried so long its weight had become a part of me, lifted. For the first time that I could remember, I felt free. Happy.

I took a deep breath and lifted my eyes to thank the dark goddess for the gift, but she was gone.

"Are you alright?" Meg asked. I blinked and looked down at her, smiling through the tears still falling freely down my cheeks.

"Yes. I've never been better."

Chapter Twenty-Four

Gareth

I couldn't even find the energy to listen to Remi's story of his encounter with Hekate. It took everything I had just to stay on my feet.

The last hour had been the worst. Something within me kept trying to drag me down, or back... somewhere that wasn't here in any case. All I could do was keep putting one foot in front of the other.

The air was stifling, so thick it was difficult to breathe. My wolf wanted to run, bolt, climb a tree. Anything to escape. Half the time I didn't know if the shuddering of my body was from sickness, or my wolf trying to break free of my human skin.

Gravity was my worst enemy. Every step felt like walking through a thick slurry of mud. My vision faded in and out, but as long as I could focus on the light of the torches ahead, I was fine. I drifted a bit, side to side, but nobody noticed. Or if they had, they hadn't said anything.

Everyone's voices were a muffled buzz in my head, and it wasn't until I felt a hand on my elbow that I stopped.

"Gareth?"

There was a pulse of power through me, pushing aside the incoherence enough for me to recognize it was Meg standing in front of me.

I swayed on my feet as I took in the extreme worry on her face. "I'm—"

The rest of the words wouldn't come. My mouth was dry and sticky, and my throat closed up.

Meg called out to someone. "Help me—"

I wasn't sure what else she said, but I felt myself being lowered to the ground.

"—spasming—"

"—needs help—"

"—how—find—can't get—"

Flashes of light and color as I fought against their attempts to move me or hold me down, whatever they were trying to do. A wordless mixture of growls and howls overtook any words I might've heard otherwise.

Why was it so cold? If I could just shift, I'd be warm again, but every time I reached for that magick, it wasn't there. Or maybe it was. Maybe I was my wolf right now.

It was impossible to know.

My body surged up as I fought to get back to my feet. We had to keep going. I wasn't going to be the one that slowed us down or ruined this mission altogether.

Something heavy landed on me and I couldn't move. The last thing I knew was Meg's face leaning over me and her cool hand on my forehead before I was pulled down into the darkness that was waiting for me.

Everything was black and all around me was the wailing of those lost souls. I heard it, felt it, tasted it. The agony. My chest split from the pain of hopelessness.

I was going to die here and be given a veil of my own, left to scream into the void until I was finally absolved and allowed to move on.

"Gareth." The deep female voice cut through the noise, louder and softer at the same time. Or maybe the other voices just gave away out of deference to her power.

This is where she finds me? At my most vulnerable, when I am unable to make my arguments to prove my worth or even speak coherent words?

"There is no need to argue," said Lady Hekate. "I have already made my decision. You just need to listen."

I floated in the darkness, searching for the source of the voice, even as the overwhelming pain and misery forced my eyes closed.

"You are arrogant, possessive, controlling. You let your base animal instincts win more often than they should, and hide behind the fact that you are a shifter. Your temper always seems to get the best of you. Even now, as I come to you to deliver judgment, you think you can argue with me. As if that was ever an option."

This wasn't going well for me, was it? The thought of never seeing Meg or my brothers again added a whole new layer to the pain. I wouldn't even get a chance to say goodbye.

"All of these qualities served you well as a leader and a commander, but you allowed them to become your entire identity, even to your detriment. And you never show any remorse, only disappointment that you can't *control* yourself. Whenever you feel you've let people down, it's not because you think you failed them. It's simply because you're embarrassed that you weren't the best."

That wasn't true, was it? I'd never thought about myself like that. Even though I had my flaws, I was conscious of them. I tried to be better. I apologized. Humility was no stranger to me, especially now. All I'd ever done had been for the people I love. For the causes I believed in. Sometimes you had to be hard, unforgiving. Cold. It was necessary to do the kind of things I'd had to do. But I'd never let that get in the way of how much I cared for people.

I'd had a much better lid on my temper ever since the outburst where I cut Meg with my claws. It had been an accident, I could never hurt her on purpose. And after that incident, the memory of it and the frightened look on her face were enough to remind me that there were more important things at stake than yelling at someone. I removed myself from any situation that might blow out of control.

I had these bad qualities. I was managing them and making sure nobody got hurt because of them. They made me stronger, more resilient.

"And yet you still can't ask for assistance. Even as your body burns with fever, you are fighting to get back to your feet. Because you don't want to admit weakness. You don't want to lose control," she said. "All of your companions would die for you, and they would certainly do everything in their power to make you well. But that would require an admission on your part that you *need* help. You will never truly be a part of that family until you can admit that you aren't a lone wolf anymore. You are part of something far greater now. No matter how many ways you find to cope with your weaknesses, with your bad traits, none of it will make any difference in the long run. Not until you let them in."

Haven't I done that? I had laid my soul bear to Meg, proclaimed my love for her.

"It still isn't enough," she said. "All the charm and charisma that you hide behind, the romantic gestures, making her your entire world. It won't save you, from yourself or their ultimate rejection of you. Because it's not sustainable. Everything you've built on the lies you tell yourself will crumble and fall. And if the family you've built is resting atop it, what do you think will happen?"

They didn't revolve around me. Nothing had been set that firmly on my shoulders. Only the responsibilities that I'd taken for myself. They were all free to do as they wished.

"Not while you are the primary mate. Meg has a soft spot for you. You will always rank the highest, even if she doesn't admit it to you, herself, or anyone else. She *is* the center of that family, and she has placed all of her hopes on you. Her security blanket. She loves the others, feels as safe with them as she does with you. But deep in the back of her mind, she will always pick you. This is something that she needs to work on for herself, but she certainly can't do that alone. She needs help from the source. And the source is unable to give it."

Even though I couldn't see her, I could feel her gaze burning me, full of scorn.

"You have helped her build her castle in the sky, and if she was forced to choose, you would be the only one given entry. And that puts all the others at stake. You were worried about causing strife within the group? Prove it. Do right by them."

Did she want me to walk away? I couldn't do that even if I tried.

She scoffed. "You still don't get it. You're still making it about *you*. Find that pack mentality, the one that you gave up on so long ago. It was a defense to save yourself back then. You have no reason to continue it now. Know the importance of allowing yourself to truly build a family. Doing so requires humility, openness, and a readiness to admit to that family that you need them. There is far more reward in that vulnerability than you will ever find in being a pillar that they've built their house around. You will all be unstoppable for the true strength being a family requires."

She paused for so long that I thought she was gone.

"I am going to give you one chance. You will be given an indeterminate amount of time, at my discretion, and if I judge that you haven't made the necessary changes, I will return for you. A more difficult lesson will need to be taught, one that I will get guaranteed results from." She smirked, or at least that's what it sounded like when she added, "Consider this next part complementary."

I woke.

Chapter Twenty-Five

Gareth

The screams and darkness were gone. My vision was back to normal, I could think clearly again, sounds were crystal.

And I was face down on the ground with a half-shifted dragon sitting on my back. The tip of his tail was curling in the dirt right in front of my eyes as he spoke quietly with the rest of the group. "Get off me," I mumbled, dirt billowing from the puffs of my breath.

Hadi paused and I could feel his weight shift as he leaned down to look at my face. Ridges of scales and spikes at his temples were the only sign of his shift that made it to his face. I really had to learn how to control the different aspects of the shift like that.

I raised one eyebrow. "Now, please," I said.

He grinned. "Gladly. You make a terrible cushion."

I turned over and stretched, every muscle sore. "Did you have to sit on me?"

"When all else fails to keep a raging werewolf down, get a dragon to sit on him," said Felix.

"Only partially," said Hadi, chuckling. He must've shifted in a hurry because his clothing was torn. He noticed me staring at it. "This is coming out of your pocket."

"Shit. We're on the hook for destroying Death's lounge, and I have to buy you a new pair of pants?"

"How are you feeling?" Meg asked, sitting next to me. I wanted so badly to bundle her in my arms and pull her into my lap, but Hekate's words still rang in my ears. I needed to figure out how to comply with her instruction, and I had a feeling not laying an immediate claim on Meg the second I saw her was a good place to start. I still wasn't entirely sure what she wanted of me, but... we'd all figure it out together, right?

"Better now," I said, taking her hand. To the group at large, I said, "I'm sorry. I should've asked for help."

"You spoke with her, didn't you?" Felix asked.

I nodded, trying to figure out exactly what I should say. I kept the explanation as succinct as possible and couldn't decide if the knowing glances and cocked eyebrows made me feel understood or annoyed.

"You didn't get a judgment, you got an assignment. She gave you homework," said Felix, snickering.

"I'm glad you got to your personal gnosis so easily," I said.

Meg wiped a hand over her face. "This is a lot to take in." She sighed. "Do you feel like you're able to keep going? We can rest here a little while longer," she said, looking around to make sure everyone agreed.

"Actually," I said, hesitating, "I do need more rest." Those were some of the hardest words I'd ever said in my life.

Remi smiled and nodded approvingly. "He's already learning."

"Or he's terrified Hekate will come back and kick his ass, right here, right now," said Felix.

Meg grimaced. "And I feel like you might be pushing your luck."

"Cheeky does it," he said.

Meg pulled a face. "You just let me know how that cosmic boot feels when it's lodged up your ass." She patted him on the shoulder and stood. "I'm going to scout ahead a little bit," she said.

"Not alone. It's not safe," said Hadi.

"I'll be fine," she said. "I'll stay on the path, and I'm not going very far." She readjusted her weapons and pulled at the collar of her shirt. "I'm crawling out of my skin, I'm so restless."

"Anything we should be worried about?" Arthur asked. "Did this feeling just start?"

Meg paused and thought about it. "Kind of. But I'm sure it's fine. It's not unusual for me." She looked around. "I can't be the only one that finds this place claustrophobic."

We all shook our heads. "Definitely not," Andrus said.

"Please be careful," said Hadi.

"Always," she said. "I'm the queen of careful."

"Watch out, Felix. She's trying to replace you as the group comedian," Remi said, albeit lovingly.

"I'd probably have been back by now if we hadn't had this whole conversation," she said with a smile, throwing her hands in the air. "I'm leaving now."

We watched her go, and I tried to ignore the worry gnawing at the pit of my stomach.

CHAPTER TWENTY-SIX

Meg

I kept fiddling with the knife strapped on my ankle. No matter what I did I could not get it to where it sat comfortably. My mates would freak out if I didn't keep this walk short, but I just had to move. I wanted to go racing forward on the trail, change into my wolf, fly so fast that the wind whipped through my hair. Hell, I would've settled for jogging in place.

It was the kind of sensation when your skin felt tight, but nothing like it does for a shift. I just needed to be somewhere else, be some*one* else. Do something stupid, or crazy, or grand. A scream at the top of your lungs for no reason kind of restless.

This would usually warrant going for a jog in my former life, back when Bel and I lived in the middle of suburbia. Timeline-wise, that was all only about a month and a half ago, but it felt like a hundred lifetimes had passed since.

What would be an apt word to describe this journey so far? Whirlwind? High-octane, thrill ride? Nothing seemed to fit.

And now here we were, in the sixth realm of hell, aiming for the gates of Tartarus at the end of our road and hopefully it wouldn't be *the end* of our road.

There was a tree up ahead that was perfectly forked, calling me to climb up. The smooth birch bark was soft under my fingertips as I braced myself for the small jump that landed me right in the middle of the fork. The tree almost seemed to sigh, glad for company, and the leaves shook without a breeze.

"It probably gets pretty lonely out here, huh?" I asked.

The leaves shook.

"Do you get many travelers through here?"

No shaking.

"How do you think we're doing so far?"

Again, the leaves shook.

"Keep your branches crossed that we make it to the end of this. And I don't get absorbed by a sentient, arcane portal before I can finish the job I was supposed to do."

The branches swayed this time, sending a shower of leaves over me. I smiled. "Thanks... I think."

"Birch trees are generally supportive," said a voice. "She's not lying, though, when she says that not many paths cut through here. This one is a special route."

"Lady Hekate," I said, bowing my head. I made to jump out of the tree, but she waved me back and instead joined me, the bow in the tree widening a bit to accommodate us side by side.

"It's good to see the trees happy." Her face was closed off as she said, "They don't get to witness a lot of pleasant things."

"Is that my warning for how this is about to go?" I asked.

She shrugged. "What do you think?"

"I think that I've done remarkably well, all things considered. I fucked up a whole lot, but I've never given up."

"Admirable qualities," she agreed. "This isn't just about what you've done with your life. It's about who you are."

"I'm an evolved version of the twelve essences that made me, forged into my own person. If we're talking the nuts and bolts of *who* I am."

Hekate looked at me, disappointed. "That's *what* you are." She sighed. "You've never realized the difference. It's possible to be both a construct and an individual. Not just embracing your nature and learning to make the best of it, hoping you can eke out some kind of life of your own. You always default to defining yourself by your beginnings. Which is easy enough to do for anyone. But you keep picking and choosing different things to attach yourself to. Whatever you think will get you the farthest away from what you perceive yourself to have been meant to be."

"I'm afraid I don't follow," I said.

"You keep riding other people's coattails, dear. First, it was every pop-punk star that you caught a glimpse of in the magazines the servants would sneak you growing up. Then it was Bel." Her lip curled in disgust. "After that, it was Gareth."

"Gareth?" I asked. "Hold on—"

"Oh, child. Don't tell me to 'hold on.' This isn't a friendly conversation we're having. I'm laying out facts."

I snapped my mouth shut, suddenly very afraid.

She shot me side-eye. "That won't be necessary either. You've passed the tests." She shifted, placing her hand against the bark of the tree. "I'm just here to share some worldly advice. It's similar to the conversation I had with him. But you won't be on probation like he is."

"You aren't going easy on me because we're related, are you?" I asked.

Her lips thinned. "Quite the opposite. Because of that fact, I have judged you more harshly than any of your mates. You have a lot to live up to, and I don't fancy having a niece out there in the world making our family look bad."

I swallowed thickly. She may have said I have nothing to fear from her, but that didn't mean I still wasn't.

The corner of her mouth twitched into a smile. "I can't say it was with flying colors, but"—she looked at me—"you've made me proud."

I met her eyes, and they were full of so much wisdom and *power,* it took my breath away.

"One day," she said. "You'll get there."

I blinked. "Sorry, what?"

"The wisdom and power. It will be yours one day."

My first thought was that she knew the Hexengate wouldn't claim me, that there was a happily ever after at the end of this.

"Assuming you make it through the challenge that waits for you in Tartarus."

She chuckled at my visible deflation. "I can't see the future. I'm simply saying what I know you're capable of." She paused. "Which brings me back to the matter of individuality."

This time I didn't argue or try to interrupt.

"You've always picked the strongest person around you to cling to. To make their strength yours. Finding the attributes that you most want to see in yourself, and emulating them like a mirror."

I clasped my hands in my lap. There might've been some truth to that.

"What I wish for you most of all is that you realize you are capable of all of these things on your own. Stop looking at yourself through the lens of other people. Stop thinking that your construct nature automatically precludes you from possessing these things on your own. I want you to look inside yourself and actually *see* what's there. Without any other preconceptions about what you *think* you might find, certainly without expectations of what you think you *should* find."

"How is that possible? To look at myself that objectively? I've been living with myself my whole life," I said, laughing at the absurdity of that statement but not knowing how else to say it.

"You'll find a way. There is great strength within you." She placed her hands over my own. "You just need to own it."

I nodded, not wanting to let her down for anything. "I will."

She smiled and her eyes crinkled at the corners. "Good."

In a blink, I was sitting by myself again, the warmth of her hands still lingering over mine. I gave the tree one more pat before heading back to the others.

"Oh, there you are," said Arthur, coming around a sharp bend in the trail. "We were starting to get nervous."

He offered his hand and I took it, stopping him. He looked back at me in confusion. "Something wrong?"

"I just wanted to ask how you've been doing? There hasn't been much of a chance to catch up and since you haven't... you know..."

"Been a damsel in distress like those other idiots?" he asked, laughing.

I snorted. "Yes."

"I'm..." He shrugged. "I won't say 'fine,' but I've had worse days."

I nodded. "Fair enough. Any luck tapping into your power again?" I didn't want to seem tactless, but at the same time, we needed to know.

He shook his head and winced. "Not yet." Still gripping my hand, he started back down the trail.

"It'll come," I said. "I truly believe it will." I chuckled. "We're not just keeping you around cuz you're a pretty face."

He blew out a breath. "That's a relief. I was starting to wonder."

"We also might have need for a good stone mason," I said, keeping my face neutral.

It took him a minute to process what I said, and then he barked a laugh. "Already making plans for Château de Meg?"

The others looked up with relieved smiles as we returned. "I just got a visit from my aunt," I said.

Under his breath, but still fully audible to everyone, Felix muttered, "I hope that's not a euphemism for something."

CHAPTER TWENTY-SEVEN

Arthur

The more I heard from each of them about their encounters with Lady Hekate, the more nervous I got. Gareth had had the hardest go so far, and to a degree, I could understand why. He was honorable to a fault, but it was easy for something like that to go to anyone's head. You can fool yourself into thinking that you're an infallible hero with a few damages here and there if people keep telling you how great you are, convincing yourself you don't need to be healed.

I was digging into every aspect of my past. What was I ashamed of? What was I worried she'd find? Or would it be more of a sad commentary, going over everything that had happened with Sasha, and what a fool I was to not see it immediately. I could've put everything in jeopardy.

All I wanted, all I had ever wanted was a family. I was denied my own growing up, stolen away to a world where I was just an accessory. Bring out the human child to do tricks at parties, or ask him questions that he couldn't possibly know the answer to and laugh at him like he's a fool.

By the time the fae family had turned me out into the wilderness, I had already learned many cruel lessons about life. I was alone for well over a decade before Felix ran across me. I was a little better than a half-feral animal at that point, just trying my best to survive.

Once Felix had gained my trust and vice versa, my entire outlook changed. I thought maybe the world wasn't filled with complete monsters. And then I met the faerie queen. Cruel and merciless, and so cold just the memory of her chills my blood. She would've been perfectly happy to see both of us dead.

If Felix hadn't begged to go with me, not only would I have failed the trials, but I wouldn't have even tried. It just would've confirmed every negative thought I've ever had about people. But instead, we became tied to each other, leaning on each other as we continued to learn all the lessons life would throw us.

When Felix had the idea to join up with a mercenary group in the human world, I couldn't believe it. I may have been born there, but I hadn't set foot outside the faerie realm since I'd been stolen away. I had never even visited the Strangefells, which ran parallel to faerie, the barrier so thin it took nothing at all to travel over other than a thought and a confident step.

But there was no question that I would go with him. We'd already been through so much, the idea of being separated was unimaginable. He really was the only thing that made me keep going, despite the fact that he was an asshole and half the time I want to kill him. But he showed me kindness when no one else had, and even when I had to fight to see it, there was goodness in him.

The mercenary group we ended up joining with was a group of ruffians that barely held itself together with the threat of violence from the most scarred and damaged man in the bunch. They had no concept of strategy, couldn't stay on track even though the paycheck depended on it. We had been chased out of as many kingdoms as we'd been hired by.

Leaving a group like that is never a small thing, never as simple as just walking away, but even though they were Strangers, they were sad examples. One night we slipped away, killing the leader in his sleep and vanishing into the darkness.

No one came after us.

We wandered, joining other groups periodically, but never committing to anyone. We traveled the world like that, and that was the first time I truly felt alive. I also became very aware of the added sense of responsibility. Humans were so fragile, every time we had dealings with them, I took it upon myself to be an advocate, make sure they weren't taken advantage of or dealt with too severely.

I bore the brunt of many jokes, but I was human too. I may have been granted a gift by the faerie queen, but it made me no more a Stranger because of it. And most Strangers would never hesitate to remind me of my roots. They would keep me around for the luck that I brought them, nothing more. They tended to assume Felix did the same, keeping his human pet around to bring him good fortune.

I didn't truly start to get worried until it became obvious how much faster I was aging than Felix was. I'd never felt my mortality until then. I didn't want to leave him behind, I didn't want to get so old that he would leave *me* behind. That panic really set in when the aches and pains of a hard life became an every day battle. My joints were constantly hurting, swelling to the point that I couldn't walk at times.

Felix would try to brush it off, make light of it. Tell me he'd have to trade me in for a new human and try to make accommodations for me magickally. Potions would work for a time, contraptions that he was able to put together forming sturdier braces for the worst of it.

But my hair grayed and my joints gnarled, my fingers becoming so misshapen that I couldn't even hold the handle of a bucket. Felix had to help me with everything. Everything. But he did. And while he joked, he never complained.

He didn't know, and I would never tell him, but on the day the Titans found us was the day I was determined to walk out into the wilderness and not come back. The dawn was cold, and it took longer than usual for me to get moving. Every step was excruciating, and I was looking forward to finding someplace quiet to be my end.

There was a fountain in the middle of the forest that we had found a week prior. We'd been on our own for some time, nobody willing to take Felix in as long as he had an elderly human in tow. I thought it would be nice to stop there, enjoy watching the sun as it caught in the water one more time.

But someone was already there.

A woman—it took me aback how tall she was, how muscular, but there was no mistaking that she was a woman—was bathing in the freezing water. The second I noticed, I turned to leave, but of course I tripped, making a horrible ruckus as I fought to get back to my feet.

By the time I did, the woman had found me. She stood there naked and unashamed, watching me like I was some great mystery she didn't understand.

"I'm sorry," I said. "I didn't mean to interrupt." I made to take a step away and my hip gave out, sending me stumbling again. She caught my arm and righted me.

"Don't be silly. You need to rest." Like she was revealing a secret I didn't know she said, "You're not well."

I laughed. I couldn't help myself, it was so absurd.

"What is funny?" she asked.

"I'm well aware that I'm not in the best of health," I said, a hint of anger in my voice that I didn't expect.

"Then won't you come sit down?" She took my elbow and guided me toward the spring, setting me down on the flat rock that had been my destination all along.

"I'm Dione," she said, pulling a simple white linen shift over her head.

"Arthur," I said, offering a slight bow of my head.

"What brings you here, Arthur?" she asked.

I chuckled. "Rest."

Dione fixed me with such a gaze that I shriveled under the severity of it. My soul had been laid bare. "A permanent rest," she said. "A bit of an oversight."

All of my humor vanished. It was obvious this woman was not human, but now I got the sense I wasn't dealing with just another Stranger either.

"Where is your companion, Arthur?" asked Dione. "Felix, I believe his name is?"

My mouth gaped open. "How do you know these things?"

"I know plenty more besides. Including how much pain you're in. And why you really came out here today."

"Is there something you wanted from me?" I asked.

"To give you a second chance," she said.

I laughed, ending on a cough that speckled my lips with blood. "I'm far past that. You won't get much use out of me anymore."

"We can find plenty for you to do. Men like you are not easy to find. And while your friend is a bit... much, he still has promise. We could use both of you for our cause."

"What cause?" I asked. "I'm a bag of bones, dead on my feet. I doubt I have a month left in me, and any of that time would be spent waiting to die."

"But it doesn't have to," she said. "You were given luck, but what if we could give you life?"

"Who is we?" I asked, a note of desperation in my voice. This all seemed too good to be true, and everything I've heard before led me to believe it was impossible. Turning back the clock on human mortality was only ever temporary. And the price you paid in the end wasn't worth the benefit.

"I am a Titan," she said.

I could only stare. It made sense, but at the same time I couldn't wrap my head around it. This woman clearly possessed something different, a power I wasn't familiar with. And there was no hint of deception. I was always pretty good at telling a lie from the truth, and being raised among fae, that was saying something.

Of course, I had heard of the Titan wars. They were so distant, all they ever were were stories. Drunk men in taverns regaling everybody with tales of their former of glory, pissed away, just like the ale they spent their last coin on.

"But why would you need a human?" I asked again. "What could I possibly have to offer?"

"Your body can be rejuvenated. It's your character that we want."

Dione walked over to me and I watched her, heart hammering in my chest. She placed her hand in the center of my chest and a wind kicked up, blowing her blond hair around her face. An energy that I could only describe as the essence of life itself flowed through me, and when it was gone, so too, were the aches and the pains.

I peered into the water and couldn't believe my eyes. I was young again, staring back into a face I hadn't seen for fifty years.

"You can walk away right now," she said. "We won't stop you. Keep your youth as a gift. What I am really offering you, though, is purpose. Something that will stop your aimless wandering."

The word was out of my mouth before I even had a chance to truly contemplate what I was getting myself into. "Yes."

Dione smiled. "Good. Go to your friend, make him the offer. Come back when he's made his choice."

And that was that. That was the beginning of the odyssey, which led me to this point.

"You were born twice, but it wasn't enough."

I turned and found Lady Hekate behind me. I thought this memory had felt a bit too real.

"You are a good man, and you needn't have worried about passing all of my tests." She appraised me. "How much more are you willing to sacrifice?"

I opened my mouth to answer, but she vanished.

CHAPTER TWENTY-EIGHT

Hadi

We were on the second day of travel. The torches were reliable companions so far, but something kept nagging at me. The others had all had their encounters with Hekate within the first day of being here. I was still waiting.

Another half a day went by, and the trees began to thin out, almost imperceptibly at first, then at a quicker pace. We could actually see the end of the path and what lay beyond.

A desert of crystalline sand, shimmering in the glow of the same starry sky that had met us upon our arrival here. One final torch sat at the end, and three black dogs stood around it.

"This is it?" I asked.

"Are you disappointed?" Gareth asked. He looked far better now that he had rest and a new perspective on life to contemplate.

I shook my head. "No. Just confused."

"About why you weren't visited?" Meg asked.

I nodded, placing my hand at the small of her back as she stood beside me.

"Maybe it's just because you're too perfect," Felix said. "You didn't even have any baggage like Remi."

We all knew that wasn't true.

"Should I be worried? Will I be able to leave with you if she hasn't passed judgment?"

"How do you know she hasn't?" Arthur asked. "She might honestly not have anything to teach you. You were a priest. You spent two thousand years with introspection and trying to find the meaning of life, right? You've done a lot of work already, maybe all of it."

"I would've expected Andrus to complain about not having something new to learn." Remi shook his head.

"When there is nothing new to learn, you must look inside yourself for the lesson." All three dogs barked and I looked over to see Lady Hekate standing with them.

I bowed at the waist. "Lady."

One side of her mouth quirked into a grin. "A proper priest of the old gods." She waved her hand. "I just came to see you off."

I shifted uncomfortably, wanting to ask, but knowing it would be a bad idea. She hadn't forgotten. If she didn't have anything to teach me, it was up to me to figure out why.

Her eyes caught mine, and I knew she had read my mind. She gave me the slightest nod.

"Do you all have the protections that Death gave you?" she asked.

I checked to make sure my necklace was still fastened securely and noticed the others do the same.

"Good. Once the seventh realm guardian realizes you aren't supposed to be there, the portal will open. With any luck"—she glanced Arthur—"it will be the shortest part of your journey."

Meg took a couple of awkward steps toward Hekate. "Lady, do you want to see your kin released?"

We all watched with bated breath as the dark mother considered. "They have been suffering relentless torture for the last several thousand years. They are resilient, but their minds are not unbreakable. What you release may not be what you expect. Be on your guard." She took a step closer to Meg. "No matter what happens, remember that they do care about you. And your mates. They don't know how to show it," she said, grinning. "But they do care. You just may need to remind them of a few things upon their release."

Meg nodded. "Thank you."

Hekate waved her hand again, and a portal appeared. A thin sound like a single-string violin screeched out of its depths.

"Good luck," said Hekate firmly.

Meg checked her weapons one more time before jumping through, and the rest of us followed.

The realm of the Forsaken was exactly as it sounded. Dark, cold, a constant threat of danger all around. Nothing ever slept here. Nothing rested. There was no peace.

It was hard to see too far ahead, but it was enough to at least be aware of any pitfalls we might literally or figuratively run into.

"Should we just stand here and wait for it to notice?" Felix asked.

"Do you really want to stand in the same place and hope that we're noticed by the right thing?" I asked.

"When you put it like that," he grumbled.

"We keep moving," I said. "Easy does it, but we don't stop."

My own words were difficult to stick to. The farther we traveled the more uncomfortable it got, like the walls were pressing it around us, a million spirits watching us. Finding a cave to hide in would've been preferable at the one-hour mark.

"Any chance you could do what Hekate suggested?" Gareth asked Arthur, who shook his head.

"I've been trying. I can grab hold of the lightest spark of luck, and it just fizzles out."

"Anybody else seeing the giant shadows that are surrounding us?" Meg asked.

"I was hoping I was just imagining those," said Andrus.

"Where?" I asked.

"They're difficult to see against the darkness, but the biggest concentration is over there," said Remi, pointing.

I followed his direction and stared into the dark, just able to discern shadows darker than their surroundings.

"We know these ones mean us harm," said Meg. "I—"

She froze, staring off into the distance. We all followed her gaze and noticed a smaller paler shape moving fast toward us.

"No," she said. "There's no way."

"Meg? What's—" Gareth cut off mid-thought and snarled. Now that the figure had moved closer, I could see why. Belsioch.

He stared behind him as he ran, perhaps not even aware that we were there. I looked around for a place to hide, hoping we could avoid his notice and therefore a fight. I didn't want him anywhere near us when that portal to Tartarus opened.

Then he spotted us, putting on more speed. Meg was frozen in place, but when he was twenty yards out, she snapped into action, grabbing the haft of one of her axes.

Belsioch stopped short. "There's no time for that. We need to go."

"Why would we bring you anywhere with us?" she asked.

"Because you aren't cruel enough to leave me here," he said, very confident in his words.

Meg scoffed. "After all that you've done? You honestly think I couldn't leave you here? If anyone is deserving of this fate, it's you."

Behind him, an entire swarm of shadows appeared, racing across the barren land toward him.

"Please!" Belsioch begged, real fear in him.

We didn't have time to waste on this encounter. The shadows were moving in fast.

"Let's go!" I said. "We'll worry about this later." If all else failed, when the portal opened, we would incapacitate him and leave him behind.

The shadows moved faster than we could outrun them, even at a jump-step pace.

"Arthur?" I asked, getting nervous. I didn't want to know what would happen if they caught up to us.

He didn't respond. I looked over and noticed that he'd stopped.

"Arthur!" I shouted.

Power spiked off him and the portal flared open, sputtering sparks and flame. The shadows screeched and pulled back but more were coming at us from all sides. We bolted for the exit, dodging the gnashing teeth and reaching claws of the forsaken.

Bel was right on our heels, but one of the ghouls grabbed him. He fought to get free but it was no use. "No!" Bel cried. "Don't leave me here!"

We kept running, ignoring his pleas.

"Why do you want to leave us?" The feminine voice came from the shadow that had hold of Belsioch.

I turned my attention back to the portal. It was so close.

There was an awful cry, a shriek from behind us. The others were through the gate now, but running feet made me turn.

Just in time for Bel to collide with me and push us both through the portal.

CHAPTER TWENTY-NINE

Meg

I turned back to the portal just in time to see Hadi come falling backward after Bel launched at him. The portal snapped closed, and silence fell, thick and heavy. All we could hear bouncing off the cavernous stone walls was our own ragged breathing.

Bel stood and looked around, relief flooding onto his face. That just wouldn't do.

I hefted my axe and stalked toward him, shoving him against the wall with the blade against his throat. "Give me one good reason I shouldn't kill you now," I said.

"I can get you through the gate," he said, confident that would be the answer that saved his life.

"We already know how to get past it," I said. His face fell.

Now that I got a close-up look at him, I could tell how much Bel had changed. That arrogant smile was replaced by a nervous grin, seeking mercy. His face was drawn, gaunt. It was his eyes that spoke the loudest. They were haunted and pled with me not to ask questions.

His entire body looked frail. Whatever had happened when I'd separated him from Legion, it had taken its toll. Or rather, its pound of flesh.

"Well? What else can you offer?" I asked.

"Just kill him," Gareth growled. "Nothing he says is worth a damn."

I understood where he was coming from, and I was sorely tempted, but now that Bel was here, maybe we could use the information he had. "He created this place. It might come in handy to keep him around."

"She's right," said Andrus. "Just in case. We don't know what we might face."

Gareth grabbed Bel around the neck and pulled his face close. "If I catch one whiff of deception, I don't care what they say. I will kill you."

Bel nodded. "Understood."

I turned away from him, looking again at the caverns that led to the gates of Tartarus. The last time I'd been here, I was chased by a dragon, a lesser creature than Hadi. It wasn't a shifter and didn't have any more basic understanding than a young child.

"This way," I said.

We all fell into step, Bel guarded between Gareth and Remi. The Ætherim didn't look any more at ease, but his fear wasn't quite so pungent.

I kept glancing at the ceiling, expecting the dragon to make an appearance. It was a guard dog after all. But when we made it all the way to the main cavern without a sighting, I looked back at Bel. "What happened to the guardian?"

Bel shrugged. "I don't know. He was fine last I left him."

That didn't give me a whole lot of confidence, but we continued. There was a sharp bend with a rocky outcrop blocking most of the view of the main gate. When we turned the corner, we halted.

Up ahead was the massive double door, behind which the Titans waited to be freed. It was exactly the same as I remembered it. What was different, though, was the entire range of demons lined up in front of it, a dragon carcass lying at their feet.

"Are these friends of yours?" I asked Bel.

He shook his head. "Not mine."

Gareth growled. "You lie. What did you do?"

Bel shot him an irritated look. "Nothing. I don't know who they are, besides the obvious."

Now I could see some of that fear melt away, the old Bel returning. He was back in territory he was familiar with.

They had all clearly seen us, but they made no move. What were they waiting for, if they weren't here at the behest of Bel?

"Just wait your turn to die." The raspy voice came from one of the demons in the front of the line. "Turn back."

I shrugged. "Okay." I went back around the corner, ushering for my mates to follow me.

I could only imagine the looks of confusion on the demon's faces.

"What's the plan?" Felix asked, looking to Andrus, the strategist, for the answer.

"There are too many of them," said Andrus. "We'll never be able to get past them with just us. And we don't want Arthur wasting any power if we can avoid it."

I grinned, looking at Bel. "What if we call up old friends?"

"Risha?" said Andrus. "She did say she would help if she could."

Gareth was already on it. I could feel him reach through time, part the layers of each reality and close them up again after he was through, leaving no trace or psychic mess behind. He was getting good.

Risha, he said.

It took a minute, but she answered, her voice carrying through all our heads courtesy of the bond.

Gareth?

How fast can you marshal the nephilim most loyal to you? He sent her a mental picture of what we were facing. *You don't have to help us beyond running interference at the gate.*

Risha paused. *I don't know... I may be on the fence, but this is a bit more direct involvement than I'd like.*

"Wait," said Felix. "Are you forgetting the very big reason that Death didn't send us here on the express line in the first place? Even if we accomplish this, do you want the wrath of the Watcher and Lady Hekate coming down on us if we just invite a bunch of friends over?"

Andrus shook his head. "This is the beauty of keeping him alive," he said, shooting Gareth a look. "Bel has the master key. It's his house, his rules... kind of. If he invites them into his own realm and opens the direct portal he uses himself, we'll be fine."

"Are you sure?"

"We don't have a whole lot of choice," I said. "I'd rather swing for the fences and be diplomatic later."

Felix couldn't argue the point. *Risha,* I said.

Meg! Are you okay?

I'm fine, but I could be better. If there's any chance you can help, we really need it.

This time there was no hesitation. *Alright. Give me twenty minutes.*

Thank you, I said, glad for the quick response time of creatures that were born and bred for battle.

Bel scoffed, a pretty bold attitude. He may have been horrified by whatever he'd seen in the Forsaken realm, but it clearly didn't have a long-term effect.

"Risha? What's she going to do? The nephilim won't obey her, or accept her as a general."

"Open the portal," I said, fingers flexing toward my axe. "Let's find out."

"Let me speak to the demons, first, at least," he said. "Maybe I can sway them."

Arthur scoffed. "And let you run off and hide behind them?"

Bel turned cold eyes on Arthur. "I've already told you, I have nothing to do with them."

"Forgive us if we don't believe a word that comes out of your mouth," I said. "Open the portal."

He glared daggers at me, and I saw the same man that he'd always been. Nothing was going to change him.

"Fine," he growled. "I'm going to need a little space."

We allowed him to walk a short distance away. He knelt on the ground and placed his hands flat. Hopefully this wouldn't require a lot of power because he clearly didn't have much to spare.

"So," he said, a sneer twisting his face as he appraised my mates. "Do you all find her serviceable?"

The shift was immediate. Distrust turned to indignation. "Shut up and open the portal," I said. I spoke over my shoulder, not taking my eyes off Bel. "Don't let him get a rise out of you."

"I wouldn't deign to try," Bel said, trying to look innocent. "You're the expert at that." He chuckled darkly. "Even I was surprised by some of the things you were willing to do in bed."

Gareth growled and took a step forward and Hadi shifted to his half-dragon form, tail thrashing the ground.

"Stop it, all of you!" I said, saving the most severe glare for Bel.

"Whenever she would return from one of her searches for you, she would be so randy we would fuck for hours. Every which way you could imagine. That's the only thing I miss about you, Meg. That sweet little pussy. Although, it's probably ruined now."

Before any of my mates could make a move, I walked up to Bel and stood in front of him, staring him down as I drew my power around me. I used to see a monster.

Now, all I saw was a pathetic weasel whose only form of control was in keeping people afraid.

And I wasn't afraid anymore.

"I know exactly who you are," I said. "I see your cowardice. You can save your stupid mind games for your shadow friends back in the Forsaken realm."

His cocksure smile faltered.

"Your time is done. There is no world in which you will ever hold power again. You could've been someone great, a name people remembered forever. And you have accomplished that. But the only reason anyone will ever speak your name now, is to utter it as a curse. You are one of the most foul beings that has ever walked this planet. Far worse than anything the Titans ever were."

I leaned in closer. "I was there, you know? In those flashbacks, time travel, I'm still not sure what it was. But I saw those memories of you as a boy. The cruelty that your father made your entire family suffer. You were capable of love. You were a mama's boy."

"Shut up," he hissed.

"But in the end, all you ever were was your father's son, waiting to pick up his mantle."

"You lie!" he shouted, reaching for my throat. I deflected his arm and flattened out my hand, jabbing it into his neck. He choked, and I followed it up with a punch to the stomach, sweeping his feet out from under him.

"You should stay down," I said. "Get used to groveling in the dirt where you belong. Now," I crouched down next to him. "Open—the fucking—portal."

Bel looked at me with such impotent hatred it made me laugh. Then he realized he had truly lost. I had been at this man's mercy, terrified of him, nightmares of the vengeance he would deliver if he ever caught me haunted me.

And now I was laughing in his face. He averted his eyes and nodded, placing his hands on the floor and calling up the gate. When it flared to life, Risha was standing on the other side of it, scores of nephilim behind her. An entire army.

Risha stepped through in full armor, and I ran to her, crushing her in a hug which she returned. The nephilim filed in behind her, many of them casting baleful looks in Bel's direction before they turned to their real leader.

When the last one was through, Bel was going to let the portal close. "Leave it," I said.

He scoffed. "You want me to just leave the back door open? Anyone can walk through."

"And walk out. That's the point. It stays open."

I motioned to two of the nephilim soldiers. "Guard him." They nodded, grabbing Bel by each arm and marching him away.

I scanned the many faces, but there was one that was missing. "Ursal?"

Risha's face fell, and she shook her head. "He's not doing great. He was one of the most invested in Bel's vision of the future." She glared at Bel but wasted no more time on him.

"What's the plan?" she asked.

We walked back over to the others.

"Good to see you again," said Andrus, clasping her hand.

"They're just waiting? None of them tried to attack you?" she asked, jerking her head in the direction of the demon army.

"No," said Remi. "They barely even acknowledged us. We just got a flippant warning from their commander."

"They want us to stay away from the gate, and that's the extent of their concern," said Arthur. "It has to be the chaos demons."

Andrus laid out a quick strategy, him and Risha going back and forth, tweaking the plan until it seemed solid.

"That was impressive," said Hadi, wrapping his arm around my waist. "What you did back there."

"It felt good," I said.

"I only know part of the story, but even that..." He gnashed his teeth. "Your control is amazing. I would've ripped his head off."

There was something else on his mind, and I waited patiently for him to say it. "I'm not sure what we're all walking into, but I want you to know—" He paused. "I'm glad you found me. Even though we were bound to wind up at the gates of hell, there's nowhere I'd rather be."

"Except maybe at home," said Felix. "After this is over. Just chilling out."

"We'll get there," I said. "We've got an army."

"And each other," said Arthur.

"Gross." Felix pulled a face.

Andrus and Risha finished up their planning and joined us. "Okay," said Andrus. "I think we've got something that'll work." He turned to me. "Risha's forces will forge a path for us, and you'll work your magick. We just need to wait for our opening."

"Once I get up there, what do I do?" I asked. "Just ask the gate to open nicely?"

Felix piped up. "Devil's advocate, hear me out."

"Shocker," Remi mumbled. Felix shot him a look, but didn't take the bait.

"Why don't we just have Bel open the gate? Wouldn't it be a lot easier?"

I shook my head. "There is nothing that would convince me he wouldn't try to twist it to his favor. He cannot be trusted. For anything." I nodded my head back at the portal. "The only reason he did that was to prove to us that he still had power."

Felix conceded the point.

"Trust your gut," said Gareth. "It hasn't led you wrong so far. You'll know what to do."

That didn't make me feel any less sick to my stomach, but we had to move. There was still a ticking clock hanging over my head.

I nodded. "Let's do it."

Chapter Thirty

Meg

My mates surrounded me, and I cobbled together something that resembled the magick I'd used on Andrus to pop his soul back into his body. In my mind's eye, I wove a mesh of thin energy lines linking all of us together.

Each strand was woven around our souls, tapping into that very core essence, a shining golden light traveling between all of us as I absorbed their essences.

None of us had any idea what to expect, but my number one fear was ripping someone's soul from their body.

"Ready?" I asked.

They all nodded, looking at me with nothing but absolute trust. I took a deep breath, and pulled, twining their souls with mine. It was a heady sensation, and all the traits I'd received from them began to manifest. A vampire's teeth, a gargoyle's skin, a wolf's claws, the golden shimmer of illusion magick, a dragon's tail and wings.

When it was done, I opened my eyes and looked around, nervous. "Everyone alright?"

They were all smiling at me. "Perfect," said Arthur.

"Woah," said Risha. I cast a glance over at her, realizing what I must look like.

"Wings?" Remi said, a huge smile spreading across his face.

"She'll be joining us in the air in no time," said Hadi.

I let myself soak in their love and comfort and calm as long as I could, but the Titans wouldn't wait.

"I guess it's time then." I nodded to Risha.

The demons guarding the door looked only a fraction more interested in our presence as we rounded the corner with an entire army at our back.

"Can't take a hint?" asked their commander.

"I would, but we really need to get to that gate," I said. "You can either move, or we move you."

The demon laughed, and all the others joined in. "I'd ask 'you and what army,' but you've already provided that answer."

He drew his sword. "You should know, though, I'll be forced to call in reinforcements if you attack. The bosses made it very clear that we were to keep you away from these gates at all costs."

I glanced behind me at the almost one-hundred-strong force Risha had brought with her. Beings that were designed for warfare. None of them looked worried.

Risha gave me a small smile. "We've got you."

"See you on the other side," I said, saying a silent prayer to whoever would listen that it would be true.

Risha gave the order and her army surged forward, charging the demons at the gate. The commander stood strong, lifting his hand. When the nephilim were within a hundred yards, the space before the gate exploded with activity. Demons of every shape and size poured out of crevices, appeared out of thin air, popped up from holes in the ground. Everything from pit demons, to imps, to the humanesque demons that made up hell's royal courts.

"Shit," I said, heart in my throat.

Risha's army never slowed, never stuttered, they kept charging into the horde of demons, and when they met, it was with a clashing of steel almost deafening as it crashed off the walls around us. Screeches and roars mingled with battle cries, and soon with shouts of pain.

"There!" said Andrus, pointing to an opening that was forming in the middle of the field.

"Here we go," I said, sprinting forward. I flapped my wings, Hadi and Remi beside me while the others charged ahead on the ground. I leaped, shouting in triumph as I caught air and Remi whooped, diving low to drive his blade through a gremlin's heart right before it could slash at Gareth.

I pumped my wings, but keeping them in tandem was a lot more difficult than Hadi made it look. I faltered and before I could recover, the air dumped from my wings, and I went hurtling toward the ground.

"Meg!" Hadi shouted, diving after me. The demons below were waiting for me, and I tried to summon the fire breath, but it wouldn't come.

A burst of fire from Hadi had the demons scattering and covering their faces and when I landed among them, they couldn't get organized fast enough. I slashed with my tail and knocked a clear path around me for Remi and Hadi to land, tucking my wings in close to my body.

We forewent the flying idea and fought our way to the others. After a quick regroup, we ran for it, pelting toward the gate. Gareth and Hadi led the way, clearing out any stragglers, while Remi and Andrus guarded our rear. I was flanked by Felix and Arthur as they cut down anyone who tried to get too close.

Hadi and Gareth parted as soon as we reached the gate, allowing me to run through them as my mates closed in a half circle around me.

I hadn't had a whole lot of time to look at the gate the last time I was here, too busy watching my back and the dragon that was hunting me. Now, as I gazed up at the incomprehensible size... how was I supposed to get this thing open? I placed my hands against the hot, stinking iron, and I could feel the flesh and blood that had been fused into it when it was forged. There was an oily residue, the kind of magick that left a bad taste in your mouth.

I closed my eyes and *felt* it, let its darkness creep over me. It tried to wrap itself around me and pull me in, but I didn't let it. I pushed back, forcing my power, my new signature and everything the Titans imbued me with into that gate, overriding the magick already there.

The ground rumbled and my mates closed rank as more attackers turned their attention to us. I had to trust that they would be okay, I had to focus on getting this done.

Debris fell from the ceiling high overhead as I pushed more of my power, feeling it race upward toward the top of the gate. Faint lines of light were forming along the currents of my magick as it flowed, almost at the top.

I sent one last massive burst into it and there was a terrible cracking noise, so loud it stilled the entire battle. The gate trembled, iron braces rending, melting. I leaped backward as molten iron ran in rivulets to the ground.

Demons scattered, running every which way, disappearing back to wherever they came from.

Cracks formed, and a low hum built in intensity. It split and shook, wobbling in the frame as the entire thing came loose and teetered toward us. I gathered power around me and blasted it at the door, pushing it back the other way. It fell with a crash and the fetid, rotten stench of Tartarus filled the air.

My mates recoiled, covering their mouths and noses as a complete and total silence fell over the chamber around us. I turned.

The demons were gone. They failed in their given mission and fucked right off. Risha's army was standing in the middle of the cavern, surrounded by the fallen of both sides. The small cadre she'd left to guard Bel was dragging him around the corner, looking confused.

Roars of victory rang out from within the chamber, and I flinched. We'd been working toward this moment. This is what we wanted. So why was my gut churning with nerves?

My mates and I looked at each other. "Now what?" I asked.

CHAPTER THIRTY-ONE

Meg

"This is as far as we go," said Risha. "I'm sorry."

"It's okay," I said. "You've already done enough." I couldn't blame them. I didn't want to walk in there either.

"We'll stay close, just in case," she said.

"Thank you." I walked forward and clasped her hands in mine.

"Good luck." Risha looked around at the men. "To all of you."

"We should bring Bel with us," I said.

Bel stiffened. "No."

"You don't have a choice," Gareth growled, grabbing Bel by the back of his neck and pushing him forward.

His voice shook as Gareth pushed him past me. He snatched up my hand. "Please, Meg—"

I stared at him. "You only have yourself to blame for this. Whatever they do to you, it won't be enough."

He dropped my hand like he'd been burned.

We stood at the threshold of Tartarus, staring into the vast landscape. There were rumblings of movement inside, gargantuan footsteps. They must have been freed from their individual tortures when the gate fell.

Kronos is not himself. Trust your instinct.

The words floated through my head. Lady Hekate? She'd said something similar, but it didn't *feel* like her.

"Everything alright?" Remi asked, leaning close.

I nodded. "Yeah." I took a deep breath and regretted it, the stench flooding my senses.

One foot in front of the other, Megiste. We've got you. We've always had you.

I froze. "Meg?" Andrus asked.

"I'm fine," I said. "It's just—"

Just what? A strange voice is speaking into my head? A voice that my bonded mates can't hear?

I looked around at them, meeting their concerned gazes. "Let's finish this."

We stepped forward.

The trek was slow in a landscape built to scale for gigantic beings. The Titans can cross a mile with one step, so even though their "special" prisons weren't that far apart by their standards, we had plenty of time to get a good look at things as we walked.

"This is what they've been suffering for two thousand years?" Felix asked, turning a sickly green.

"It was even worse to actually see them in it," I said, voice choking at the memory.

We all looked at Bel who cowered under the glares, before straightening and trying to wrap his superiority back around him. "I did what I thought was best."

No-one bothered to reply.

There were sounds up ahead, voices, grunts of pain, harsh laughter. When everything else was entombed in eerie stillness, those sounds were all the more terrifying.

I led the way up the hill in the center and as we crested the top there were general murmurs of disgust as my mates realized what we were standing in.

"Kronos was kept here," I said, staring at the churned puddle of filth and broken bits of metal now missing its prisoner.

"You took your time to think these 'punishments' over, didn't you?" Gareth asked Bel.

Before Bel could give whatever pathetic answer he was going to try to sell, Hadi interrupted. "Over there."

Following his gaze, we saw a few of the Titans huddled together, helping one of their own out of his personalized torture. Hyperion, the Titan overseeing the heavens and keeping a watchful eye on the universe, now blinded and fumbling. Even as we watched, his steps became more confident, and he roared triumphantly as his sight healed and returned.

Bel shook and flinched away at the sound, would have bolted if Gareth didn't have a tight grip on him.

A sudden screech made us turn in the opposite direction. The rest of the Titans were dragging a figure between them, kicking and screaming.

"Zader," said Bel, no more than a whisper.

They dragged him over to the others as he fought against them, every attempt at escape useless. He might as well have been a baby bird flapping its wings against a hurricane wind.

Pallas and Kronos threw him down on the ground and there was a single mewl of fear as they descended. I slapped a hand over my mouth to cover my gasp as the Titans tore Zader apart with their bare hands.

All twelve of them looked up at the same time, noticing us standing on the hilltop.

Steady. The voice whispered in my mind. *We're here.*

The Titans, my family, my creators, took quick strides to us.

I wanted to run. My knees were shaking. Despite the surety and strength in the voice's tone, I was afraid.

Something's changed, said Arthur through the bond. *They aren't the same.*

The ground shook under our feet as they climbed the hill, and soon we were surrounded by twelve towering Titans.

Kronos smiled, but it didn't have the same warmth as before. "You did it."

I nodded, taking a second to compose myself so my voice wouldn't waver. "Yes. You didn't leave us with any choice. That Hexengate was a pretty dirty trick."

He shrugged. "We'd be fools not to have a backup plan."

"I told you I'd figure it out. I—"

"That doesn't matter," said Kronos. "What matters is that you are here. You've freed us." He chuckled and his tone took on the equivalent of a pat on the head for the little hysterical girl. "There will be plenty of time for you to be mad, but not now. We'll have the conversation this deserves later."

My cheeks burned at the dismissal, fists clenching at my sides.

"Is the Hexengate going to stay closed?" I asked.

Kronos pursed his lips. "You are safe from it, if that's what you're worried about."

"I'm *worried* about everyone else that's going to get caught in the crossfire if that thing opens," I snapped. "You know, the world that you claimed to care about?"

Kronos straightened, lifting his head and staring at us down his nose. "Do not speak of things that you know nothing about."

"Then why don't we all go grab a coffee and talk about it then?" I said, throwing my arms in the air. "Because certainly you aren't about to do something that would confirm everybody's beliefs about you." I wasn't backing down.

"Like what?" Kronos asked, lifting one eyebrow.

"Like going bats and destroying everything in sight!" I took a step forward and while it was ludicrous—I was barely the size of Kronos's little toe—I felt the power in it. And so did he. "Don't play dumb with me! That shit is over! I freed you because I had faith in you!"

"And to avoid your own destruction," boomed Kronos, narrowing his eyes. "Don't pretend your motivations are purely selfless."

"Because you gave me no choice!" I screamed. A burst of power flew from me in my anger and pushed Kronos back a step.

We all froze in surprise. Shit. I could feel the mood turning sourer as they realized I could be an actual threat. Only problem was, I didn't know how to repeat the process, or even if I could.

"Hand over Belsioch," Kronos said, puffing out his chest.

Still looking shocked and confused, Gareth pushed Bel forward. He tripped and landed face-first in the muck at Kronos's feet. He looked so small and broken. My heart raced as the true surreality of this venture hit me.

It wasn't a mistake. Trust us.

"Easy for you to say," I mumbled, realizing too late I'd spoken out loud.

My mates gave me quizzical looks, but I shook my head.

The Titans surrounded Bel, and the rest of us backed up, not wanting to be anywhere near him when the Titans exacted whatever vengeance they pleased. I told myself to keep watching, no matter what they did.

Rhea began to chant, words of a language long forgotten that even the lexicon was having a hard time translating, and I gasped.

Bel was growing and shifting, taking on his full Ætherim form, but the look on his face made it clear it was causing him great pain.

"What are you doing?" I shouted. What purpose could they possibly have for restoring him?

Kronos flicked his eyes toward me and back to Bel. "Taking back our power."

Bel cackled, staring up at the king of the Titans with disdain, holding on to his false bravado even when he was at their mercy. "What power? You have none. It's all been siphoned away the instant you call any. Even now, it eludes you. It's how this place was designed."

The smile that slowly spread across Kronos's face froze my blood.

"That was the point," he said. "We expended too much power warring with you and your kin. We couldn't finish it on our terms. So we surrendered. Let you"—he held up his finger—"*let* you lock us away. The accommodations were less than pleasant, but it gave us plenty of time to rebuild our power."

"You went through all this for *that!?*" I shouted. "To end it on *your terms*? What happened to watching out for the little guy? What happened to protecting people from power-hungry lunatics?" I heard the desperation in my voice and hated myself for it. They'd fooled us all. He'd played me. Kronos had appealed to my vulnerable side, offering a loving, supportive family. A place to belong. And I'd bought it, hook, line and sinker.

"We can protect the people best by ruling them," he said, cold and heartless.

I fell back a step, and my mates surrounded me, the bond burning with our collective fury and sense of ultimate betrayal.

Kronos raised his hand and all the shards of every crown that he'd been forced to crawl over rose from the filth, forging themselves into a giant golden sword.

"Now we just need the key to crack open the siphon."

I only realized what he meant to do a second before he did it. "Wait!"

Bel also saw what was coming, flinching away as Kronos plunged the sword through the center of his chest. Bel's face was a rictus of shock as his body spasmed, pinned to the ground.

Nothing happened.

We waited, holding our breath and gazing around.

A pulse of light formed over Bel's body before shooting downward, where there was a great boom that shook the earth.

Dread crept over me. It started slow, that fountain of power working its way back up the path the light had just made. Just a small trickle. Completely controllable.

And then the tap opened all the way.

A geyser of power sprang up from Bel's body, burning it up as it went.

"Back!" Hadi shouted, all of us running down the hill as the Titans stood on their island, a growing ocean of power at their feet. I looked back once we reached the bottom.

Kronos had madness in his eyes.

CHAPTER THIRTY-TWO

Meg

"We need to get out of here," said Felix.

"There's no place safe to go!" I shouted. "Not now!"

Gareth took me by the shoulders, forcing me to look away from the Titans. "Let's at least get clear. Then we can figure out what to do."

"Meg!" Risha's bellow came from the entrance, and we all turned.

"Fuck!" My hand went to my axe and the others drew their own weapons. While we'd been busy with the impending doom before us, what seemed like the entire rank of chaos demons had been materializing behind us.

They were massive, almost as big as the Titans themselves in their full manifestations. At least a dozen of them, only a handful of which I could name. Leviathan, Behemoth, Jormungandr, Apophis... no Legion, so I guess at least they were still out of the game.

Behemoth moved forward, his lumbering gait almost like a limp. His massive body was covered in dark, oily hair. He might've resembled a bear if not for the serpentine tail and the elongated head, caught somewhere between canine and reptile.

When he spoke from a mouth that was never made to form words, I felt sick. "Stay out of our way and you may live."

I took a step forward. "Why are you here? Your shot at the Hexengate is over."

Behemoth grumbled. "That may be so, but that isn't the only prize to be had." His red eyes traveled to the ocean of energy still rising from the ground, being slowly drawn in by the Titans.

This just kept getting better and better.

Guard yourself, Megiste, said the voice. I only had to wonder what she meant for a brief instant before I felt a tug in my center that stole my breath away.

I looked down. A glow was emanating from my chest, a dull pain along with it.

"What's happening?" Felix asked, panicked.

"I don't—" I screamed as the pain flared, blasting spots across my vision and sending me to my knees. Felix, Andrus, and Remi crouched next to me while the others formed a protective guard.

"Gods," Arthur whispered. "They're taking their power back."

Through bleary eyes, I turned and noticed a faint line of what looked like smoke drawing off my body and back to the Titans.

They were trying to destroy me.

Close it down, said the voice. *We'll help you.*

"How?" I ground out through clenched teeth.

A sensation washed over me, warm and close. A new presence had joined us and my own power rose up, triggered to life. It closed around me like a shield and the Titans' draw was immediately shut off.

"Stop fighting it, Megiste," Kronos called. "It will be easier this way."

I stood, bolstered by my mates and the mysterious new arrival, whose presence was fading away even as I regained my strength.

"Go to hell," I spat.

He raised an eyebrow. "Is that any way to talk to your father?"

Rage flared. "Don't you fucking dare!" I shouted. My magick surged forward, that same force that pushed Kronos back last time, only bigger. All twelve Titans staggered back and judging by the sounds behind me, the chaos demons did, too.

Bind the power, said the voice.

I lashed out, weaving my magick into the ebb and flow of that fountain of energy, treating it like an entity, exactly like I'd done to twine the souls of my mates to me earlier.

I let a portion of my magick sink down and with a jerking motion of my hands, I cut the font off at the source. Kronos roared in fury and tried to draw faster on the power already loosed, but it wouldn't respond to him anymore. He lunged toward me, anger contorting his face, but I lashed out, blasting him back again and freezing him and the others in place best I could.

But it was too much. I was already straining to contain the power, and the geyser underneath us was pushing against the blockade with immense force. With my concentration divided, I couldn't hold the Titans for long either.

"I can't let any of them get it," I said. Sweat beaded on my forehead and my whole body shook from the effort.

"It's going to tear you apart!" Andrus shouted. "You have to let it go!"

"No!"

The chaos demons made their move, lunging forward. Hadi transformed into his dragon. He was small compared to the rest of them, but it was an advantage nonetheless.

I let out a relieved cry as Risha's army joined the fray. I couldn't help them. I had to figure out what to do. I couldn't hold it, they *couldn't* have it. What did that leave?

CHAPTER THIRTY-THREE

Arthur

The truth was inescapable. We were losing. My power had returned, but it kept failing to manifest in any but the smallest ways. Ducking at the right time, pushing someone out of the way, arranging for one of the demons to get caught up in the attack of another. We swarmed the chaos demons like ants just trying not to get squashed but dealt no real blows.

I looked back at Meg. She was weakening, her whole body visibly shaking from the effort. She couldn't hold it much longer. She'd let the power destroy her before she gave it up.

The eerie sight was the kind that would burn itself into the memory of generations. A small figure on one side of an ocean of power and twelve mighty Titans on the other shore, striving to overtake one woman alone.

And she was not backing down.

This couldn't fail. We *couldn't* fail.

I watched with horror as my brothers' energy waned, their movements losing their usual grace and deadliness. They all bore bloody wounds, and more were dealt before they could heal the old ones.

You were born twice. But it wasn't enough. Those were Hekate's words.

Now they were starting to make sense.

I'd gotten a second chance at life, but it wasn't for me. It was for them. I wasn't meant to stay.

I ran to Meg, my luck magick the only thing that kept a wild swing from a giant club from pulverizing me and instead smashing into the side of the demon's head about to make a snack out of Andrus.

"Meg!" I shouted.

"I can't hold it back much longer. Get the others out of here," she pleaded.

"Where would we go?" I asked. "If we die, we die together." But if this went according to plan, that wouldn't be the case. Not for all of us. "Let me help you."

"How?" she asked, quivering so badly I thought she would collapse. One of her knees buckled and I caught her arm. The power coursing through her jumped to me as well, and in that moment, I was floored that she was still standing.

It felt like liquid fire, glass shards, hot pokers, grains of sand, needles, all of it jammed through my veins with a hurricane force. The pain was overwhelming. My skin burned where it touched her.

And she knew. In that moment, she read exactly what I planned to do.

"No," she said, shaking her head. "You can't." Tears were already forming in her eyes. "There has to be another way."

"Yes, I can," I said, my word final. There was no argument to be made.

I reached through the bond and opened the floodgates, pouring all of my luck into her. It brought with it a different kind of pain as my life force drained out of me with it, crashing against the blistering rage of the Titans and forming a blissful in-between.

Meg glowed, brighter than the pure energy in front of her, a supernova about to reach critical mass.

About half my luck was gone, and so was the pain. The world faded as I focused solely on the two of us.

"You will win," I said, lifting my hand to her face. "This is the gift I was always supposed to give. I know you won't let it go to waste."

"Please," she whispered. The grief on her face was enough to make my heart stop prematurely before it thudded painfully and carried on. "We just got you back. You can't leave."

"I'm not leaving. I'm returning. I'll be okay. And so will all of you."

She leaned into my touch, turning her head to kiss the palm of my hand. It was almost time.

"I'm sorry," she said.

"I'm not." I smiled. "I got to see my brothers again. I was able to fulfill my purpose. And I will die, knowing that I loved you."

A sob tore from her throat and I rested my forehead against hers. "As much of my heart as there is to give, you have it, Megiste."

The last dregs of luck passed from me to her.

"And you have all of mine," she said.

The sweetest last words to hear.

CHAPTER THIRTY-FOUR

Meg

"And you have all of mine." I was crying so hard, the words were barely distinguishable. The last of Arthur's power transferred to me. A sweet, peaceful smile spread across his face before his entire body was engulfed in shimmering golden flame.

I didn't flinch away as he burned, the fire so hot that within seconds, he was gone. Not even ash was left.

I screamed, long and loud. I stared across the distance at the Titans, smug smiles on their faces as they simply waited for me to tire and die.

Arthur's magick hummed in my blood, fueled by the building rage that put all fear I felt to shame.

This would end on *my* terms. The Titans would yield.

Then the idea came to me. "I have to give it to someone else," I said to no-one, the plot already forming in my mind.

Fate wasn't out of this game yet.

"Protect them," I whispered, a small prayer for my mates and friends.

I couldn't travel through the realms under my own power and still hold the Titans back, so I called to Time, hoping he was still on my side even though he and Kronos had a much deeper history. When he answered, I felt hope.

Kronos's eyes went wide as he felt Time draw near. The smile grew on his face, until he realized his old friend wasn't coming to help him.

"No!" he screamed, just as a portal opened up and a hand appeared to yank me through. There was a blinding flash, and I was gone.

Back to the Fates.

"Thank you," I said, as Time left me.

I stood in that quiet chamber, looking at the desiccated corpses of the three women. "Please let this work," I said.

The energy source in Tartarus was still bound to me, and I slowly drew on it, approaching the Fates with caution and reverence. That presence I'd felt earlier was stronger here.

"It was you, wasn't it?" I asked, a small smile twisting my lips.

I carefully removed the desiccated eyes from the spindle and placed them in the empty sockets, letting instinct—or maybe the ghosts of the Fates—guide me as to which one belonged to who.

I wove the stream of time around the Fates and flooded the power into it, encasing them in a bubble. If I simply turned back the clock, all I would be left with were fresh corpses. Restoring their lives would take a lot more, and as luck would have it...

I let myself become a channel, letting the energy flow through me without trying to control it. I infused that bubble with the raw, primordial power while shuffling time backward. Their mummified bodies became decomposing corpses, turned to freshly dead bodies with fresh wounds, still bleeding.

I slowed time, right to the point where they died, and in that moment, I poured all the energy coursing through that bubble into those bodies, healing them. The wounds disappeared, both eyes were restored, but there was no sign of life.

The power trickled away and I faintly registered that I'd used almost all the Titans' reserve.

"I don't understand," I said, approaching them. "It should have worked. Why didn't it work?"

You must call us back. Our souls need to be summoned. We're too far away.

"How do I do that?"

You can't. Death can.

I immediately called out for Death and there was a crack in the air as he appeared. He took one look at me and then at the Fates and sighed. "Going well, is it?"

"They need you to call their souls back. They said they're too far away to return on their own."

Death chewed his cheek, thinking. "You don't ask for much, do you?"

"If anyone can do it..."

He crossed his arms. "They shouldn't even exist anymore. They were killed by chaos demons. It should have been oblivion."

"They seemed confident you could make it happen."

Death blinked. "Have you been speaking to them?"

"Sure seems like it. I can't imagine chaos demons would want me to bring the Fates back, right?"

Place your hands on his head.

"Um."

"What?" He narrowed his eyes.

I smiled sheepishly and reached for his forehead. Death leaned back as if repelled by a magnet.

He held up a finger. "I repeat. What?"

"They want me to put my hands on your head."

He stared at me and huffed. "Fine."

I reached out and he recoiled as soon as my hands touched him. "Come on," I said.

"They're clammy. It caught me by surprise."

"We don't have time for this!" I snapped.

He nodded and stood still. I reached out again and set my hands on his forehead. A rush of visions passed through my mind, and I heard Death gasp as he saw them too. A vast expanse of stars, entire galaxies, oceans of vapor and dust.

Just as suddenly as they started, they ceased, and I blinked back into my current surroundings. "What was that?" I asked.

A slow smile crept across his face. "Genius."

He disappeared. Minutes passed and I worried my lip as I waited. How long would this take? What was happening back in Tartarus right now? The Titans shouldn't have that much power to draw on anymore, but they were plenty dangerous without it and I couldn't stand not knowing.

Then I felt it. The presences of the Fates got stronger and for the first time I felt their individual souls. All three of them. Every torch in the place burst into flame, casting a warm, comforting glow and in that flickering light I watched as the Fate's chests rose and fell, intermittently at first, but picking up a normal rhythm. Then their eyes opened.

Death reappeared, shivering, ice formed on his nice suit.

"Where did you have to go?" I asked.

"All the way to the heavens. Bloody freezing out there."

My mouth fell open in shock. "Beg pardon?"

"There are more things in heaven and Earth than are dreamt of, yada, yada," he said, waving the question off. "Maybe some other time."

The Fates were taking stock of their surroundings, moving their bodies slowly as they got used to being back. Atropos grasped her sister's hands and they bowed their heads toward each other, whispering quietly.

The urgency to return to my mates hit me hard as I watched them.

Sensing my unrest, they all turned to me, kind smiles spreading across their faces.

"We need to get back to Tartarus," I said. "The Titans have lost their minds."

"Joy," said Death, his shoulders sinking a bit.

"Don't worry about them, leave them to me," I said.

Death's eyebrows rose at my confidence, but he didn't say anything.

"But we could use your help with the chaos demons running amok."

"Of course they are." Death straightened his suit coat, the remaining ice flaking off and cracking on the floor. "My dear Fates," he said, pausing. "We will return?"

They dipped their heads. "There is much we need to discuss," said Lachesis.

I cast one more look at the Fates, trying not to become overwhelmed by their presence. I tore my eyes away. "Bel's dead—"

"Oo," said Death, clasping his hands in front of his heart. "You should've led with that."

"—but his portal should still be open."

"Direct shot, got it," said Death. He grinned at me. "You look properly terrifying by the way."

"The Titans are about to find out how terrifying," I said, voice low and dangerous.

The Fates each raised a hand in farewell. "Go," said Atropos.

Clotho placed a finger atop her wheel. "We'll have your back."

With a small push, the wheel began to spin.

The portal was fading but we were still able to cross through it. We took off running toward the main chamber and I never thought I'd be happy about hearing the ongoing sounds of battle.

"I take it you haven't figured those out yet?" Death asked, motioning to my wings.

"What? Oh, no. Not yet."

The threshold of Tartarus was directly ahead of us now and my heart leapt into my throat as I saw the Titans fully engaged in the battle.

"No!" I put on a burst of speed and Death was right beside me.

Bodies littered the ground, chaos demons and nephilim both. The Titans were engaged with the demons, but there were only a handful left standing.

I saw Gareth and Andrus fighting back to back. Remi, wings torn and bloodied was barely standing as he helped Risha and a few of her nephilim tackle a wounded Apophis. Felix kept popping in and out of view, confusing the demon he was battling into a frenzy that made it easier for the nephilim to deal significant blows.

Behemoth turned and spotted us, surrounded by a vanguard of nephilim. He'd taken heavy hits, but it was clear the nephilim didn't stand much of a chance of taking him down alone.

Death was grinning like a madman and the sight struck me to the point that I stopped and watched as he stalked to Behemoth, showing no outward aggression.

Behemoth swung his tail and Death just stood there, letting it hit him. He sailed backward, and just before he smacked into a wall, he stopped, hovering in midair.

His grin only got wider and more terrifying, and Behemoth noticed it, too.

"My turn." Death moved in and the nephilim scattered out of his way. Darkness was roiling off his shoulders like living shadow and black lightning gathered in his hands, sparking and crackling.

I could feel the power shift in the room, a denseness in the air almost like heavy humidity combined with an electrical storm.

"Oh, shit," was all I could say, right before Death blasted Behemoth with such a force, the chaos demon was blown back, tumbling into a heap. Death hit him again and the smell of ozone and burnt flesh filled the air as Behemoth screeched.

The battles all around us had come to an end as we watched Death deal the final blow. Every hair on my body rose on end as a wave of power broke over Behemoth, Death laughing hysterically as the demon thrashed and screamed before igniting in a brilliant flash of fire that seared across my skin.

I turned away, shielding my eyes, and when I looked back, Behemoth was gone.

The remaining chaos demons didn't wait around to meet the same fate. Between the Titans and an angry egregore, they knew they didn't stand a chance. In a flash, they too were gone, but unlike the brethren they left behind, they'd live to fight another day.

Any relief I felt quickly disappeared as I noticed—

"Hadi!" I screamed, running toward his prone body. He was back in his human form, and he wasn't moving.

"Meg, wait!" shouted Death.

I ran to my dragon, heedless of everything else and I was lifted off my feet, like I'd been caught in a giant spider web.

Magick flowed around and through me, an ancient force I'd never felt before. My form reverted to normal, pressured by this magick, but the change wasn't as painless as it typically was. Now, my body fought the shift, and every nerve ending was screaming at me as my body morphed its shape.

"Meg!" This time, the shout came from Gareth.

The force suspending me in the air spun me around until I didn't know which way was up or down. I jerked to a halt.

Face to face with Kronos.

Distantly, I could hear my mates calling for me. Blinding pain shot through my head, overriding our bond, as my maker sifted through my thoughts.

"What are you looking for?" I asked, words slurred as the pain made me want to vomit. "I'll gladly tell you all about how shitty a parent you are."

"What did you do with it?" he snarled. The other Titans were all gathered around us.

"Your power is gone," I said, smiling. "I used it all."

"Lies," he hissed. His anger sliced through me with agonizing pain.

"No." The word was a whisper. "You're the one creeping through my head. You know I'm telling the truth."

"Kronos?" Pallas asked.

The king of the Titans kept rifling through my brain, looking for an answer he liked better. He didn't find one.

He roared so loud the cavern shook. "You stupid girl!"

The world spun and I realized Kronos was shrinking down to average human size, until I was standing across from someone only a few feet taller than me.

The magick binding me backed off and dumped me on the ground. Before I could pick myself up, Kronos lurched forward and grabbed the shoulder of my armor, hauling me to my feet. The other Titans crowded around.

"What have you done?" Kronos stared at me with wild eyes, bloodshot and not even close to rational.

"What I had to," I replied. The soul ties I'd formed with my mates were still holding strong. For what I had to do next, I hoped they stayed that way.

He was shaking with rage. "Why would you betray us like this?"

I paused, shocked. Then I burst out laughing. "Are you joking?"

At the open-mouthed confusion on his face, it was clear that he wasn't, and I laughed even harder. I searched for the ties that had bound us together as creators and construct. They'd each given a part of themselves to form me. One by one, I identified each piece of myself that wasn't actually me and I hoped that Arthur's luck would come through one more time.

"I didn't betray *you*! *You* betrayed all of *us*!"

"Megiste—"

"No! You listen!"

Kronos growled and narrowed his eyes, but let me speak.

"I *hated* you. For most of my life, I wanted nothing more than to see you destroyed. The *only* good thing that you've ever done, that I can see anyway, is choosing those men to be your captains."

"You can't speak to anything from those times," he said, low and dangerous.

"Maybe not. But those men," I said, pointing to my mates, trying not to let my gaze linger too much on Hadi. He was covered in so much blood.

"Those men thought you were heroes. Saviors. They worshipped you and your mission. Every time I had my doubts, they would convince me I only had one side of the story and not to judge you too harshly."

I shrugged. "For what it's worth, I hope this isn't your fault. You've suffered so much." I cast a look at Gareth and Andrus as they watched, terrified and helpless. "And legend has it that you gave up the best parts of yourselves for me."

Kronos narrowed his eyes. "What are you aiming at?"

"I'm giving them back."

Chapter Thirty-Five

Meg

It should have killed me. A construct separated from the power that made it, by all rights, should cease to exist.

I released the twelve bits of essence that were bound together and forged into a construct a hundred years ago, in the form of a baby girl. Sent to the Underworld in the care of a monstrous family and raised as a means to an end instead of a person.

"Rescued" by a mad god, put through trials and tortures, blessed with six wonderful mates and cursed with heartbreak so soon after she thought she'd finally found her true family.

Those events happened *to* me, but they didn't define me, any more than the pieces each Titan contributed to my making did. All of the experiences combined to make me something other. I wasn't the same Meg as when I began this journey. I'd been building my long-coveted autonomy each day I drew breath.

And now Arthur's sacrifice was not only helping me realize it, but if this worked the way I hoped...

The Titans, crowding around me with various looks of hate and anger, faltered. Their postures relaxed. Their faces softened. I could see realization dawning in their eyes as they regained those missing pieces of themselves.

There was a long moment of complete silence where I didn't dare breathe.

"Megiste?" Kronos asked. "Is it you?"

My voice broke and my smile trembled at the edges. "Yeah. We made it."

I took a step and stumbled as the weakness in my body caught up to me. Kronos caught me. A deep, jolly laugh burst from him as he lifted me off my feet and crushed me in a bear hug.

When he set me down, I hurried over to Hadi, my mates following.

"Is he alive?" Andrus asked.

His signature was weak, but it was there. I nodded. "Barely."

Kronos crouched down and laid a hand on Hadi's chest. Indigo light glowed over the dragon's body and the worst of the injuries began to knit together, but Kronos pulled back, shaking his head. "That's all I can manage right now, but his body should be able to handle the rest."

"Thank you," I said, standing and being immediately enveloped into the waiting arms of my mates.

"Arthur?" Felix asked.

I shook my head, tears starting anew.

"He sacrificed himself, so we wouldn't fail," said Felix.

"Yes," I said. "I'm so sorry, Felix."

His eyes brimmed with tears but instead of pulling away, he wrapped his arms around me and buried his face in the crook of my neck. "He really was the best of us."

Risha survived, along with only a quarter of the force she'd brought with her. After we saw them safely through the portal, it gave up once and for all and blinked out of existence. Somehow, that felt... right. Bel was gone and now that last vestige of his power was too.

Once Hadi regained consciousness, we were ready to move.

"Are we really going home?" Remi asked, wistful.

"Not quite yet," I said. "There's a stop we need to make in between."

"Does this have something to do with where you disappeared to?" Andrus asked.

"Scaring the piss out of all of us, I might add," said Gareth.

I looked at Kronos and the others, who had been helping where they could but mostly just staying out of the way. There would be no easy way for them to transition back into a normal life, or even a semblance of it.

"I'd like to show you what happened to all that raw power," I said.

The Titans agreed and walked over to join us.

"I still have a lot to take care of here, but I'll join you when I can," said Death.

I nodded and took a breath, taking Kronos's hand. He was surprised at first, but gently closed his hand around mine. "Are you ready to leave this place?"

A serene and blissful smile was my answer, one that was shared by the others.

"After you."

Clotho, Lachesis and Atropos were waiting for us when we stepped through time into their lair.

Hadi was on his feet, but allowed Gareth and Felix to support him.

"Good to see you restored," said Clotho, bowing her head deeply at the Titans. She turned to me and smiled. "Well done, Megiste. With everything." She motioned for us to follow.

The Fates led us through to the next chamber, which turned out to be a cozy sitting room. They hadn't wasted any time getting this place back up to snuff.

"Please, sit."

I feel the need to mention how surreal it is to be sitting casually in a room with twelve—although human sized—incredibly imposing Titans, five battle-worn men, and three, recently-returned-from-the-dead Fates.

"We'll try to explain things from our perspective as well as we can, but feel free to ask whatever questions you need," said Lachesis.

Atropos began. "I guess I'll start where you know it all went wrong." She motioned back toward the chamber with the wheel, where their mummies had stood for a thousand years or more. "When the chaos demons came for us, it wasn't a surprise. We'd been resisting them, foiling them when we could. But they were too powerful. And they had plenty of others under their sway that didn't dare try to fight back."

Clotho took over. "So we started to make contingency plans. There were so many threads that still needed to be woven—"

I gasped loudly, and she paused. I blushed as all eyes turned to me.

"S-sorry," I said.

"You're realizing a few things about the techniques you've been using in your magick," said Lachesis.

I nodded. "Threads. Weaving. That's exactly how I'd describe what I did in Tartarus. Both to weave my soul with my mates and to forge the connection that allowed me to return the pieces of the Titans they'd used to create me."

"One of our biggest contingencies was to ensure our power wouldn't be lost when we were separated from our bodies," said Atropos. "We did that by entwining our own Fates with others. There are people across the worlds whose paths we thought would be most likely to lead them here. You were one of them, Megiste."

"But how did the demons not interfere?" I asked. "They were still the ones guiding my creation, weren't they?"

Lachesis snorted. "They are a lot of things, but humble isn't one. Or all that smart, considering. They didn't even think we'd be capable of something like that, let alone that it would affect them in any way. They may have given you form, but that's where it ended." She looked thoughtful. "Although, there is something to be said for how much chaos follows you. There were a few times where we weren't sure if the meager help we could offer along the way would be enough. The best we could do on most occasions was to twist chance in your favor."

"Unfortunately, it *wasn't* enough, and one of your own had to make a great sacrifice," said Atropos. "I am sorry for that."

Felix made a noise but stopped himself before he spoke. "Please," said Lachesis.

"Arthur's magick being what it was. It wasn't a coincidence that he survived the Dark Forest, was it? Or that we met? Or that—"

"The faerie queen gifted him that luck when you survived the trials?" Clotho finished. "No. It wasn't."

"I still can't believe he's gone," said Felix. "We barely had any time with him."

"And the time we did was… fraught," said Gareth, wincing with guilt.

"Before he died, he said"—my voice cracked—"he didn't have any regrets. That he was glad he got to see all of you again. And he was proud to fulfill his purpose."

"We never intended for things to end this way," said Theia, Titan of the sky and ether. Sadness and regret twisted her features. "And then *we* tried to kill you."

I'd be lying if I said some part of me didn't still suspect the Titans were putting on airs, but since most of their power had been depleted and the Fates were truly back at the helm, the odds were in favor of the Strangefells if they decided to try anything again.

And we have you, said Remi, speaking into my mind.

Our warrior queen, agreed Gareth.

I was taken aback, not by their reading of my thoughts—even though I really needed to get better at shielding—but by their willingness to admit we might need to go toe-to-toe with the Titans again in the future. They were keeping an open mind to the potential for treachery.

Someone cleared their throat, and we looked over to see that Death had joined us. "I don't want to interrupt, but I don't think you should count Arthur as gone just yet."

"What do you mean?" I asked, hope kindling.

"I believe a certain lord of the underworld offered you a boon."

"But there's no body left for him to return to," Andrus said.

Death gave us a one-shoulder shrug. "Who knows. Maybe we'll get lucky."

Epilogue

We'd ultimately ended up spending days with the Fates in their realm. There were so many long-sought-after answers and even more questions, my head was still spinning as it tried to process it all.

After that, we'd gone to stay with Death while we looked for a place to call home. To start our lives together. And we still had hope that Hades could make our family whole.

It had been two months, and there was still no word on Arthur. Hades balked at the request a bit, but with Death offering assistance and the Fates vowing their help, I believed them all when they said they'd do everything in their power to try. I'd already seen what the combined forces of those beings could do, so my hopes were high. All of ours were.

"Look out!" I shouted, as my wings failed on the dive in. Andrus and Remi ducked as I went tumbling overhead, the former already having caught a wing to the face once trying to be noble.

Hadi sped by me, turning and snapping his wings out to halt his descent as he caught me midair.

He chuckled as he set me on my feet. "You'll get it. Landing is always hardest."

Felix appeared out the back door, stepping onto the patio. We'd found a nice house on the water, not that far from Death's neighborhood in the Strangefells. We all felt more comfortable with it, as the modern human world was a lot to adjust to. We could take things slower here, and the slightly less convenient nature of life in the Strangefells was a small price to pay to live in comfort with my mates.

Felix held up a sheaf of papers. "We finally got word. Accords are in the works. Select leaders from the Ætherim and the High Council will be meeting to draw their lines in the sand with the Titans."

He scooped me up in a one-armed hug and kissed me. "Guess who the guest of honor is?"

My stomach rolled. "No."

He grinned. "Yes. You, my dear, are requested to attend. With your cadre of extremely sexy consorts in tow, of course.

"Is this even necessary?" I asked. Just thinking about being in a room with all those people... "The Titans aren't nearly as powerful. They don't pose much of a threat."

Hadi grinned. "To most of the world, just the thought of the Titans brings back memories of war and strife, of towering figures half-obscured in the clouds."

"That's a bit of a reach," said Andrus.

"Tall tales get bigger over time," said Remi. His wings were still too damaged to fly for long distances, and Leviathan had dealt him some nasty wounds that still hadn't healed completely. Frankly, it's a miracle he's recovering as fast as he is.

"And even with their power diminished, eventually they could regain it all. They just need to keep waiting it out," said Felix. "Best to make friends with them now. Oh, and Gareth sent word." My eyes shot up to Felix's and the fae grinned. "He's returning tomorrow."

Butterflies exploded in my stomach. Gareth left almost as soon as we'd gotten settled, determined to follow through on Lady Hekate's lessons. It was good for both of us, that distance, learning where and how we were depending too heavily on the mere presence of the other, but it had been difficult.

"Come on," said Remi, scooping me up in his arms. "Let's go take your mind off those nervous feelings, shall we?"

He headed inside, making for our playroom. We all had individual bedrooms, and for the most part we kept those for sleeping and cuddling only. The playroom, however, was where there was plenty of space for pretty much anything and it was easier to set clear boundaries and expectations.

A small *snick* caught my attention, along with the hum of magick.

"Wait," I said, putting my hand on Remi's chest. "Did you hear something?"

"Yeah," he said, turning.

Andrus doubled back and peeked into the living room. "It sounded like the snap of a portal."

Hadi checked around the other rooms, confused. "There's nothing. We definitely heard something."

The squeaky floorboard in the kitchen sounded and we all jerked toward it. Remi set me down, freeing us both up for a fight, just in case.

I reached out for the signature to check who it was...

And I ran.

"Meg!" The others followed close behind.

I pelted down the hall, around the corner, and—

There he was. "Arthur?"

I could barely believe it. The others stopped short in the doorway, staring, just as shocked as I was.

He was right there, looking whole and perfect and... alive. A broad smile split his face.

We stood there for a moment, staring at each other in shock and joy and a bunch of other emotions all twisted up together. The bond sang as the missing piece returned and made it whole again.

Arthur *whooped* and caught me up in his arms, spinning us around. He beamed down at me before kissing me until I was dizzy. "Third time's a charm."

The others surrounded us, and I let myself get lost in the happiness of the moment. Our family was complete.

Our future together was bright.

I finally felt like I was right where I belonged.

Dear Reader

Thank you so much for reading! It means the world to me that you shared your time with the Strangefells universe. Have a moment? I'd love it if you could leave a review. It's immensely helpful for indie creators like me. Have questions or comments? I'd love to hear from you!

Reach out at author@gwydionroyce.com and let me know what you think! Or get fun extras and stay in the loop on everything I've got coming up at gwydionroyce.com

The Catalog

The Death's Left Hand Series:
(Dark Paranormal Urban Fantasy)
Book 1: Iron-Forge Crossroads: Metanoia
Book 2: Iron-Forge Crossroads: Remeant
Book 3: Coiled Phantoms: Exuvia
Book 4: Coiled Phantoms: Kairos

***

The Primordial Embers Series:
(Reverse Harem Dark Fantasy Romance)
Book 1: Trickster's Ashes
Book 2: Illusion Razed
Book 3: Stone Captive
Book 4 : Enemies Remade
Book 5: Primordial Fall
Book 6: Chaos Ending